*Maybe she'd caught some kind
of country fever, Clair thought.*

Some kind of country fever that was making her body react to things she shouldn't even be aware of. Or maybe it was *cowboy* fever, she amended. For her gaze seemed to be fixated on Jace Brimley. Cowboy boots, jeans, denim jacket, red Henley shirt, white crewneck T-shirt. Still, it wasn't the clothes that got to Clair. It was the way the clothes fit him.

The T-shirt molded to impressive pectorals. The waist-length denim jacket was stretched to its limits by the breadth of shoulders and the expanse of Jace's muscular arms. And the jeans...oh, the jeans! They were just snug enough to cup a derriere to die for.

Clair's mouth went dry, her heart thumping. *Country* fever or *cowboy* fever—she forced her eyes off Jace's rear just before he spun around.

He nodded toward his black truck and said, "Hope you don't mind sittin' in the middle. The baby's car seat has to be on the passenger's side."

No, she didn't mind sitting in the middle. It was how close she was going to be to Jace that she didn't know how to handle....

Dear Reader,

Around this time of year, everyone reflects on what it is that they're thankful for. For reader favorite Susan Mallery, the friendships she's made since becoming a writer have made a difference in her life. Bestselling author Sherryl Woods is thankful for the letters from readers—"It means so much to know that a particular story has touched someone's soul." And popular author Janis Reams Hudson is thankful "for the readers who spend their hard-earned money to buy my books."

I'm thankful to have such a talented group of writers in the Silhouette Special Edition line, and the authors appearing this month are no exception! In *Wrangling the Redhead* by Sherryl Woods, find out if the heroine's celebrity status gets in the way of true love.... Also don't miss *The Sheik and the Runaway Princess* by Susan Mallery, in which the Prince of Thieves kidnaps a princess...and simultaneously steals her heart!

When the heroine claims her late sister's child, she finds the child's guardian—and possibly the perfect man—in *Baby Be Mine* by Victoria Pade. And when a handsome horse breeder turns out to be a spy enlisted to expose the next heiress to the Haskell fortune, will he find an impostor or the real McCoy in *The Missing Heir* by Jane Toombs? In Ann Roth's *Father of the Year,* should this single dad keep his new nanny...or make her his wife? And the sparks fly when a man discovers his secret baby daughter left on his doorstep...which leads to a marriage of convenience in Janis Reams Hudson's *Daughter on His Doorstep.*

I hope you enjoy all these wonderful novels by some of the most talented authors in the genre. Best wishes to you and your family for a very happy and healthy Thanksgiving!

Best,

Karen Taylor Richman
Senior Editor

Please address questions and book requests to:
Silhouette Reader Service
U.S.. 3010 Walden Ave., P.O. Box 1325, Buffalo, NY 14269
Canadian: P.O. Box 609, Fort Erie, Ont. L2A 5X3

Baby Be Mine

VICTORIA PADE

SPECIAL EDITION™

Published by Silhouette Books

America's Publisher of Contemporary Romance

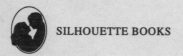 SILHOUETTE BOOKS

ISBN 0-373-24431-2

BABY BE MINE

Books by Victoria Pade

Silhouette Special Edition

Breaking Every Rule #402
Divine Decadence #473
Shades and Shadows #502
Shelter from the Storm #527
Twice Shy #558
Something Special #600
Out on a Limb #629
The Right Time #689
Over Easy #710
Amazing Gracie #752
Hello Again #778
Unmarried with Children #852
Cowboy's Kin #923
Baby My Baby #946
Cowboy's Kiss #970
Mom for Hire #1057
Cowboy's Lady #1106
Cowboy's Love #1159
The Cowboy's Ideal Wife #1185
Baby Love #1249
Cowboy's Caress #1311
The Cowboy's Gift-Wrapped Bride #1365
Cowboy's Baby #1389
Baby Be Mine #1431

*A Ranching Family

Silhouette Books

World's Most Eligible Bachelors
Wyoming Wrangler

Montana Mavericks:
  Wed in Whitehorn
The Marriage Bargain

The Coltons
From Boss to Bridegroom

VICTORIA PADE

is a bestselling author of both historical and contemporary romance fiction, and mother of two energetic daughters, Cori and Erin. Although she enjoys her chosen career as a novelist, she occasionally laments that she has never traveled farther from her Colorado home than Disneyland, instead spending all her spare time plugging away at her computer. She takes breaks from writing by indulging in her favorite hobby—eating chocolate.

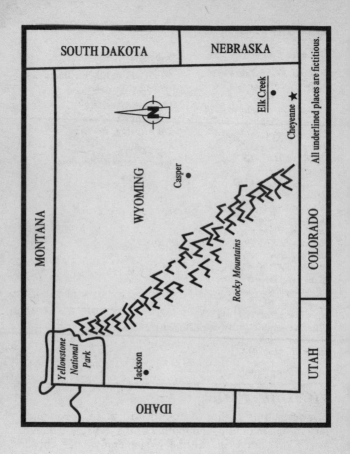

Chapter One

Clair Fletcher eased her rental car onto the shoulder of the deserted country road and came to a stop. She wanted to check the map the rental agency had given her to make sure she was going in the right direction, since it seemed as though she should have reached her destination by now.

She was in Wyoming, headed to some hole-in-the-wall called Elk Creek—hardly where she would ordinarily have gone for her vacation. Of course she wouldn't ordinarily have taken a week of her vacation at the beginning of March, either.

But this was not a recreational trip. She was on a quest.

According to the map she was still on course, and Elk Creek was only another four or five miles up the road.

Good, she thought as she refolded the map and tried to ignore the jittery feeling that suddenly hit her stomach. It was the same jittery feeling she got every time she was on her way to a big client to give a presentation. No matter how great her idea for that client's newest ad campaign, she always suffered an attack of nerves right before facing them.

But suffering those jitters wouldn't stop her now any more than the prepresentation jitters stopped her at any other time. Clair Fletcher hadn't become one of Chicago's most recognized advertising account executives by letting things stop her.

She pulled her car back onto the road and pressed the gas pedal with renewed determination.

I'll make things right, Kristin, she swore—the same vow she'd made over and over again since learning that her much younger sister had been killed in an apartment fire.

Clair barely had a basic overview of what had happened to Kristin in the past three years, and even that basic overview had come to her only a few weeks ago. Before that, Clair hadn't so much as known where Kristin was, let alone that her sister had been pregnant when Clair had last seen her. And she hadn't known that Kristin had given the baby up for adoption. Clair felt she had only herself to blame for that alienation.

If Kristin's son's adoptive parents—Bill and Kim Miller—hadn't been killed in a car accident, Clair would likely never have known about Kristin's death at all. It was only due to the fact that in the Millers' will they'd requested that, in the event of both their deaths, William's birth mother be the first person offered the opportunity to raise him. Apparently acting on behalf of the will's executor, the attorney overseeing the will had dispatched someone to find Kristin, and when that someone had discovered that she, too, was dead, the executor of the will had opted for having Kristin's family notified in case they didn't know.

Notified. That was all. Clair and her father had been notified of Kristin's death as a simple courtesy. It didn't mean her family was left with any rights to her son.

In fact, they might not even have learned she *had* a son except that the attorney had assumed the family knew and had taken it upon himself to reassure them that arrangements had been made in the will for William's guardianship and that he was being well cared for.

That's where the man Clair was looking for came into the picture.

Clair didn't know much about him other than his name, that he lived in Elk Creek, Wyoming, and that he was now her nephew's legal guardian. But three sudden, untimely deaths were leading her to him. Two accidents, one of which had cost her her sister.

I'm so, so sorry, Kristin. But I promise I'll make things right for your William. I won't leave him to a stranger. I promise....

A sign announced Elk Creek just before Clair slowed down and passed a train station that looked like something out of an old Western movie. White gingerbread trim decorated the gables of the yellow stationhouse as well as the roof that covered the passenger platform.

From there she passed a place that proclaimed itself The Buckin' Bronco, Elk Creek's Only Honky-Tonk. Then she was on Center Street where the Old West theme continued.

Quaint buildings lined both sides of a road so wide there was room for two lanes of traffic and angle parking. Well-kept shops stood along boardwalks dotted with tall Victorian streetlights. Some of the buildings were wood, some brick. None was taller than three stories, and most were only one or two.

Clair's only company on the wide street was one truck and a horse-drawn wagon, both of them moving at about the same slow pace.

It was the kind of town, she thought, where she might spend a holiday weekend browsing through the shops for handcrafted knickknacks and antiques to escape the work-week rat race.

But this wasn't a holiday weekend, and she wasn't there for pleasure. She had a mission. So when she stopped at the general store she barely noticed the sweet cinnamon scent of the place or the warmth given off by the pot-bellied stove that chased away the wintry chill outside.

The woman behind the counter smiled at her and said a cheery hello as Clair approached. Clair could tell by the curiosity in the other woman's expression that she knew most people who came through the door and was surprised to see someone she didn't recognize.

Small Town, America, Clair thought, realizing she wasn't impervious to its romanticized appeal and mentally storing the picturesque details of the place. It would come in handy for her next campaign for homemade jam or country lemonade or farm-fresh poultry.

"I'm looking for someone named Jace Brimley," Clair informed the woman behind the counter after returning her greeting. "I don't suppose you could help me with that, could you?"

The woman laughed. "I can't tell you exactly where he is this second, but I can give you the likeliest choices." She went on to recite an address for a house on Maple Street and instructions on how to get there. Then she gave directions to a ranch just outside of town, as well. "I'd try the house first," the other woman suggested when she'd finished.

Clair could tell she was curious about the reason for the inquiry, and she felt the urge to reward the other woman's friendly assistance with an explanation. But this wasn't a subject she wanted to share with a stranger, so instead she mercly asked if there was a rest room she could use.

The other woman didn't seem offended by Clair's reluctance to fill her in and pointed out the rest room without so much as a raised eyebrow to show displeasure over the fact that Clair was obviously not going to buy anything.

"Thank you," Clair said, heading down an aisle that offered a surprisingly varied selection of grocery items.

The rest room was a single, small room that could

have been the bathroom in any home except for the lack of a shower or tub. It was spotlessly clean, and the liquid soap in a bottle had a hand-lettered label that read Mom's Berry Bright Soap.

It was bright all right—bright purple—and smelled of berries. It was certainly nicer than the industrial-smelling stuff in most public rest rooms.

When she'd dried her hands, Clair took a quick check of her appearance in the mirror.

She didn't think she looked too much the worse for wear, considering that it was nearly five o'clock in the afternoon and she'd left for the airport at six that morning. Six Chicago time—four in Wyoming.

For the sake of convenience she kept her naturally curly hair very short, so it required only some fluffing with her fingers to put the bounce back into it. Her hair was a dark, burnished red, a blend of dark brown and red. The trouble was on days like today, when stress and weariness began to show, her usually pale skin seemed almost ghostly against the double-strength hair color.

Since her blush was packed in her suitcase, she opted for pinching her high cheekbones in an attempt to add a little natural color, but she didn't think it helped much.

At least her mascara hadn't run—that was a good thing—so her light-green eyes still had some definition. And she did have lipstick in her purse to freshen lips that people had told her had a Cupie doll curve.

Once she'd done all she could with her face and hair, she glanced down at the gray slacks, white blouse and gray blazer she had on. She flicked a speck of lint from her left sleeve, tugged on the collar of her blouse to straighten it and smoothed the wrinkles that sitting had put in her trousers.

Then, as if she were going to war, she straightened her shoulders and marched out of the rest room.

"I'm Kansas Heller, by the way," the woman behind the counter said as she saw Clair coming.

"Clair Fletcher," Clair responded reflexively.

She wasn't sure how it was possible, but from the look on Kansas Heller's face Clair had the impression that between giving her name and having asked for Jace Brimley earlier, she'd just told the other woman all she needed to know.

It was unsettling to think that the other woman—no matter how nice—might be privy to things about her sister or her nephew or their situation that even Clair didn't know. She was almost tempted to ask what was going through the woman's mind or to question her about Jace Brimley, but in the end she just thanked her for the use of the rest room and returned to her car.

Dusk was falling by then, and the Victorian streetlights had come on, lending a white glow to the dimness.

Clair wondered suddenly if Kansas Heller might call ahead and warn Jace Brimley that she was coming. If he might duck out rather than wait for her.

But she rejected the idea. After all, he had every legal right on his side. Why should he bolt?

The jitters got worse, anyway, though, and she felt

an increased urgency to find him. So she backed out of the parking spot in a hurry and drove faster than she probably should have up Center Street in the direction she'd been told to go.

It didn't take long to reach the keyhole Kansas Heller had described at the northernmost end of Center Street where a redbrick building and a steepled church stood. Clair rounded the town square nestled within the keyhole and turned on Maple Street where she counted houses until she reached the fifth from the corner, a small two-level saltbox painted beige, shuttered in cocoa brown, with a big front porch where a swing hung by chains at one end.

There was a light on in the picture window at one side of the oversize front door. The top half of the front door was an oval of etched glass, and some light shone through that, too, encouraging Clair to stop, since it looked as if someone was there.

Once she was parked at the curb, she got out and locked her doors before approaching the place.

She climbed the four steps to the front porch, breathing deeply to calm those persistent jitters, and rang the doorbell. It chimed loudly enough for her to hear even outside as she tried to peek through the etched glass in the door for a preview of the man she'd come to see. But the design of flowers and leaves was so intricate that she couldn't make out anything but colors and distorted shapes.

She did, however, see movement a moment after the doorbell had sounded.

And then, without so much as a Who's there? the

door opened, and on the other side was a mountain of a man.

Clair's earlier thought about him bolting became instantly ludicrous. Her bet was that this was not a man who had ever run from anything.

And why should he? His size alone made him an imposing figure.

He stood there, at least an inch over six feet tall, on legs as thick and sturdy as tree trunks. His broad chest tapered to a waist and hips that were shaped by taut, lean muscle. His shoulders were wide. His biceps bulged enough to stretch out the short sleeves of the white T-shirt he wore. And if just the sight of his body wasn't enough to tie Clair's tongue, one glimpse of his face was.

He had a look that advertisers would clamor for—sharply defined jawline; sensuous lips with a devilish quirk to the corners; a straight patrician nose; deep-set, penetrating eyes the same blue-denim color as the low-slung, faded jeans he wore; full brows; and light brown hair the shade of golden oak, close-cropped to a head that was perfectly shaped.

"Can I help you?" he asked when she still hadn't found her voice. His was a lush baritone—kind, curious and confident.

But before she could answer him, a tiny boy ran up from behind him, grabbed one of his massive thighs as if it were a pole and swung around it to land on his foot with a joyous giggle.

"I tace you!"

The big, strapping, handsome man looked down at

the little boy dressed almost identically except that the T-shirt the boy was wearing was red-striped and long-sleeved. Then he bent over, lifted the child as if he weighed no more than a small sack of rice and hoisted him to his shoulders to straddle his neck.

"I know you chased me," the big man said, hanging onto the boy's knees as if they were sweater sleeves dangling over his shoulders.

Then the man turned his attention back to Clair, waiting expectantly for an answer to his question.

"I'm looking for Jace Brimley."

"That'd be me," he said without hesitation and also without any indication that he'd been warned of her imminent arrival.

But Clair hardly heard him as her gaze locked on the little boy.

She'd been ten years old when Kristin was born, so she had vivid memories of her sister as a child. And the little boy was the spitting image of Kristin at that same age. Dark-green eyes, carrot-red hair that stuck out in an unruly brush all around his head, chubby cheeks, a turned-up nose and a deep dimple just above the left side of the same Cupie-doll mouth Clair had.

Sudden tears flooded her eyes and caught in her throat as she saw her late sister in the little boy. As she realized that he was flesh and blood—*her* flesh and blood. As he became real to her suddenly.

But she was still standing on Jace Brimley's porch, beneath the scrutiny of those denim-blue eyes, and she knew she had to say something. So she blinked away the tears, swallowed hard and said, "I'm Clair Fletcher. Kristin Fletcher was my sister."

"Ah," he said, nodding his head and dispelling any doubts she might have had that he wouldn't know who her sister had been. Who *she* was. "Come on in," he invited then, as casually as if she'd come to check out a piano he had for sale. Certainly he wasn't unnerved at all by her appearance at his door.

He stepped out of the way to allow her access, and Clair went in.

It was a cozy house. The entryway was small, with stairs straight ahead and a choice of going right into the living room or left into what appeared to be a den.

She didn't choose. She merely waited for her host to let her know where to go from there, wondering if he might leave her standing in the foyer rather than offer more comfortable surroundings.

"Hang on a minute," the big man said amiably enough as he closed the front door, flipped on a light in the den and took his charge into the other room.

"Changed my mind, Willy. You can watch the *Barney* tape now, before supper."

On went the television and then, from what Clair surmised, the *Barney* tape, before Jace Brimley returned.

When he did he pointed toward the living room. "We can go in there," he said, waiting politely for Clair to precede him.

The living room was cluttered with a large fleece-lined suede coat and a much smaller, heavy parka thrown over one end of a brown plaid sofa. Toys were scattered over the matching chair, the oval coffee table and even the hearth of the rustic brick fireplace and the second television that faced the couch.

Her host gathered up enough of the clutter to free the chair for her to sit on and one end of the couch for himself, depositing his armload on top of the coats at the other end.

Then he sat down and leveled his striking blue eyes at her. "I'm sorry for your loss."

"Thank you," she said quietly, suffering a twinge of guilt, as if she didn't have the right to accept his condolences. "I appreciated that the executor of the will informed us of Kristin's death," she continued in spite of her own feelings. "We—my father and I— had no idea where she was or what she was doing, let alone that she'd been killed in a fire. We might never have known."

"I figured as much. I knew she was on the outs with her family from before Willy was born. Thought that still might be the case."

"So you're the executor of the will, too?"

He nodded solemnly. Obviously, it wasn't a chore he relished.

"And you knew my sister?"

"We all got to know her. She lived here during the second half of her pregnancy."

"Oh." There was so much more Clair wanted to know, but now didn't seem like the time to ask. Especially not when Jace Brimley was obviously waiting for her to explain why she was there.

"I…we…didn't know Kristin was pregnant when

she disappeared," Clair began in order to oblige him. "The fact that she had a child came as quite a surprise."

"I imagine so."

"There are things that happened with Kristin that I regret. But…well…she was my sister and I loved her. And now that I know about my nephew, I…"

Clair wasn't sure how to put this. She doubted that Jace Brimley would merely give the child over to her upon request, so she'd decided that easing into the idea was a better course of action. Besides, she wanted the toddler to become familiar with her before she got into any custody issues. And hopefully while that was happening, she would also be able to convince Jace Brimley that William should be raised by a blood relative.

A blood relative who had failed his mother and wanted desperately to make up for it.

But William's guardian didn't need to know that part of it.

Clair finally settled on, "I want to be a part of his life. I want him to be a part of my life."

The big man sitting across from her nodded somewhat tentatively, Clair thought. But if he had any reservations, they didn't sound in his voice when he said, "Okay. If I were you I'd feel the same way."

Clair relaxed slightly at that response and thought that she could chalk up having reached first base.

"I've taken some time off work," she told him then. "I thought I'd stay in town for now, to get acquainted. If you'll point me in the direction of a hotel, I'll get myself a room and we can make arrangements

for me to see William.'' She nodded in the direction
of the den and added, ''I don't think he even noticed
me tonight.''

''He takes a while to warm up to people,'' Jace said.
''But as for a hotel, the closest thing Elk Creek has to
one of those is the boarding house. But I happen to
know it's full up. I have an extra room here, but it
wouldn't be proper for you to stay in the house with
Willy and me. I'll tell you what, though, our minister's
sister lives next door by herself. She might put you up
in her guest room. Then you'd be close by.''

That statement was so full of things that surprised
Clair that it took her a moment to work through it all—
from Jace Brimley's old-fashioned courtliness and his
willingness to let her into his and William's life so
easily, to the fact that he was also helping her find a
place to stay.

''The woman next door would actually open her
house to a total stranger?'' she finally asked.

''It's done around here when the need arises. My
mom would take you in, but then you'd have to share
one bathroom with her and my four brothers, plus
you'd be farther away from Willy. So we'll call Rennie first. I'm sure there won't be a problem.''

He got up then and disappeared through a connect-
ing door into what Clair glimpsed as the kitchen. Then
he came back, dialing a cordless phone along the way.

Clair was a city girl, and until she heard the ease
with which Jace Brimley persuaded the woman he'd
called to let Clair stay with her, she didn't believe

anyone would do such a thing. But less than two minutes later he hung up and turned back to her.

"It's all set. Rennie's glad to have the company."

"Just like that? Without knowing me from Adam? What if I'm a crazed serial killer or something?"

That made him smile, and if she'd thought he was good-looking before, it was nothing compared with how he looked when that sculpted face was lit with amusement.

"Are you a serial killer?" he asked with a laugh that creased the corners of his eyes and drew very sexy lines down the center of each cheek.

"Not on my good days. But still..."

"I don't think she's worried. She said for you to go on over and she'd get you settled in. Then tomorrow— if you're interested—you can come out to the ranch with Willy and me. Start gettin' to know him. Lettin' him get to know you."

"I'd like that."

Since there didn't seem to be any more to say, Clair stood and headed for the door.

Her host reached it before she did and opened it for her. "Rennie's place is just to the right. Rennie Jennings. You'll like her. She's great."

For no reason Clair understood, she suddenly searched his expression and analyzed his tone, wondering much more than she should have if there was affection for the other woman in either.

But she couldn't tell if there was more between Jace Brimley and Rennie Jennings than neighborliness, and she was just left wondering and feeling something oddly—and inappropriately—like jealousy.

She tamped it down and pushed aside the very notion that she might care whether Jace Brimley was involved with his neighbor, and said, "Thanks for not slamming the door in my face."

His square brow wrinkled in a confused frown. "Why would I have done that?"

Clair shrugged. "Someone else might have. They might not have welcomed my showing up out of the blue. Horning in."

"Lives have room for a lot of people in them. I don't see any harm in Willy knowin' he has an aunt who cares enough to come all the way from Chicago to see him."

It was a nice way to look at things, and Clair was grateful for it. She also felt a little guilty for having ulterior motives.

But she only smiled and kept the truth to herself.

"We usually get out of here pretty early, but seein' as how we'll have company, why don't you come back at nine?" he suggested.

"Nine it is," Clair agreed as she stepped back out onto the porch.

"I'd walk you over to Rennie's, but if I drag this boy away from *Barney* we'll have a half hour fit on our hands."

"It's all right. It's enough that you arranged for a place for me to stay. I can introduce myself."

"Tomorrow at nine, then. Come comfortable."

"Tomorrow at nine," she repeated.

And with that she said good-night and went back to her car to get her suitcase.

Jace Brimley didn't go into the house then, though. He stayed on the porch, watching her until she'd rung the bell on the house next door.

As Clair waited for the bell to be answered she marveled at what she'd found in this particular small town. A shopkeeper friendly enough to introduce herself, a man who hadn't balked at all at her sudden appearance in his life and instead had found her a place to stay so she could be near her nephew, and a woman willing to open her home to a total stranger.

In comparison to what she was used to, Clair felt as though she'd just landed on another planet.

And in comparison to other men she knew—less polite, less considerate, more threatened, and much, much less gorgeous—Jace Brimley seemed like something from another world, too.

But she wasn't there to be impressed by Jace Brimley, she reminded herself as she heard Rennie Jennings coming to the door.

She was there to connect with her nephew. To convince Jace Brimley that she should be the person to raise William.

And that was exactly what she intended to do.

Chapter Two

Willy didn't do it every morning, but he did it often enough that Jace didn't even open his eyes when he felt the little boy get into bed with him. He didn't have to look at the clock to know it was about 4:00 a.m., either. When Willy got into bed with him it was always about 4:00 a.m.

Jace didn't mind.

He was lying on his back, his hands on his chest, and he just stretched one arm up and out along the second pillow so that the toddler could burrow into his side like a pup looking for warmth.

It made him smile, and once Willy was situated and settled, Jace gazed down at him.

Yep, there he was, curled up to him as close as he could get, sound asleep again, one index finger poked through his security washcloth to rub it methodically against his chubby cheek.

Jace didn't really understand the appeal of the washcloth. He knew some kids got attached to blankets and stuffed toys, but a washcloth? He couldn't figure that one out. It had been a stocking-stuffer the year before last—a washcloth with a big, goofy-looking Rudolph the Red-Nosed Reindeer on it. Kim had said that Willy wouldn't go down for a nap or a night's sleep without it, and for a while after the accident he hadn't let go of it for a single minute.

But now he was back to just wanting it to sleep with, and that felt like an accomplishment to Jace, as if he'd been able to return Willy to the same sense of love and safety the little boy had felt with his mom and dad.

Jace pulled the covers up over the child, rubbed his head as if he really were a puppy snuggled up to him and waited to fall back to sleep himself.

But that didn't happen as easily as it usually did. Just the way it hadn't happened earlier in the night. And for the same reason.

Clair Fletcher.

Jace just wasn't too sure what to make of her and her sudden appearance in Elk Creek.

She'd said she wanted to be a part of Willy's life and she wanted Willy to be a part of hers. A simple enough statement. But what exactly did it mean? Did it mean she wanted to be someone who visited him now and then, who maybe had him visit her occasionally? Someone who talked to him on the phone to keep up with him, and sent him gifts for birthdays and holidays?

Or did it mean something more than that?

That's the part that had Jace on the alert. Because the truth was, his gut instinct told him that she'd meant more than that.

He didn't have anything tangible on which to base his doubts. But he'd seen her eyes well up with tears when she'd taken her first real look at the boy, and for a minute Jace had thought she might actually reach out, snatch Willy and run with him. From that moment on Jace had had a strong sense that she'd come to claim Willy for herself.

But if that was true, she was in for a rude awakening. Because Jace wasn't going to let that happen. No matter what she might think, he wasn't giving Willy up. Not only had he been granted legal guardianship through his best friend's will, but he'd made a pact with Billy Miller the day Billy's adoption of Willy had become final. A pact that if anything ever happened to Billy, Jace would take over for him and raise the boy. And Jace didn't take that lightly.

Besides, he had been more than happy to step up to the plate. He'd been so closely involved with Willy, even before Billy's and Kim's deaths, that Willy had seemed like his own son. He'd been Uncle Jace, who baby-sat and brought gifts, who played with Willy and took him on outings to the ranch. Uncle Jace who'd discovered through those tiny tastes of parenthood that he had a pretty strong urge to become a father himself.

Unfortunately, the desire to become a parent was

not shared by the woman who had been his wife at the time, so instead of looking forward to having a child of his own when Billy and Kim had died, he'd been trying to put a divorce behind him.

But that was all over now. And he might not have a child of his own making, but he had Willy and he intended to concentrate on being the best dad he could be to the boy.

Sure, he supposed Clair Fletcher could complicate that, if she had a mind to, but she wasn't going to change it. He'd do whatever he had to do to go on raising the boy, even if it meant war.

It would be too bad if it came to that, though, he thought. Not only didn't he want a custody battle with her, but there were a whole lot more pleasurable things he could think of to do with her....

An image of her drifted into his mind's eye, that first image of her when he'd opened the door to find her standing on the porch. No, thoughts of custody battles had definitely not been what she'd initially inspired in him.

She was damn beautiful. A knock-out—that had been what he was thinking when she'd said her name and he'd suddenly recognized the resemblance to Kristin and Willy.

Her hair was darker than theirs. Richer. It didn't have the pumpkin shades of her sister's hair or her nephew's, it was the red of cherry wood. And it was a stark frame to the color of her skin. Flawless, porcelain skin so luminous it almost hadn't looked real in the porch light.

Her eyes were something, too. Big, wide, green eyes, so light they were like looking at meadow grass through spring frost.

And there was sure nothing wrong with the rest of her. Delicate features—a thin nose, high cheekbones, lips so soft looking and so sweetly curved, the only thing they could be called was kissable.

Plus, her body—what he'd been able to see of it through the opening in the coat she'd never taken off—was great. She had long legs for a relatively short person—he guessed her to be not more than five foot three or four. Small hips and waist. Just the right size breasts...

Oh, yeah, she was not at all hard on the eyes.

But that didn't make any difference, he reminded himself. Willy was his priority. Raising Willy. And regardless of what Clair Fletcher had on her mind, raising Willy was exactly what he was going to do.

Cherry-wood-colored hair and stunning green eyes or no, Jace swore to himself that he would keep the lovely Miss Fletcher at arm's length—at arm's length and in his sights so there wouldn't be any surprises from her.

And that was all there was to it.

Except that even with his determination in place, it was still hard to get her out of his head....

As Clair stared into her open suitcase trying to decide what to wear to the ranch, she realized that her options were limited.

She'd only packed one pair of blue jeans, so that

narrowed that choice. But what to wear with them was more difficult since she wasn't sure how dirty she might get.

She opted for the oldest sweater she'd brought with her—a hunter-green V-neck that she wore with a white T-shirt underneath—in case it was ruined.

Once that decision was made and the clothes were laid out on the bed, she took a shower and shampooed her hair, all the while trying once again to calm those familiar jitters in her stomach.

The cause was two-fold today—thoughts of Jace Brimley and thoughts of Willy—as her nephew was apparently called.

Although it wasn't something Clair would ever admit to Jace, she'd never been much of a kid person. Not that she didn't like kids. She did. She just hadn't had very much experience with them.

She'd baby-sat for Kristin. Their ten-year age difference had made her perfect for that. But her younger sister had been the only child with whom Clair had had contact. And that had been a long time ago. So she wasn't altogether sure how to relate to Willy. How to make friends with him. How to get him to warm up to her. Especially when he seemed to have been totally oblivious to her the previous evening, during the brief time before he'd been dispatched to watch his *Barney* tape.

Would he even notice she was there today? And if he didn't, how would she draw his attention? Because she needed to have his attention. She needed him to like her. She needed to win him over. If she could accomplish that, she'd have a firmer footing to stand on when she put in her bid to take custody of him from Jace Brimley.

Jace Brimley. Another cause of her jitters.

Clair didn't like not being perfectly honest and up-front with him. She wasn't a deceptive person, and practicing even a small deceit made her uncomfortable. But even if she hadn't been sure before, she knew that after seeing Jace with Willy last night, he wouldn't just give her the little boy for the asking.

In fact, she was convinced that if she'd been open and aboveboard about why she was really in Elk Creek, Jace wouldn't have welcomed her the way he had or allowed her free access to Willy. That would have kept her from bonding with her nephew the way she hoped to and would have left her on shakier ground both in getting Jace to agree amicably to give the boy over to her and in winning any court battle, if it came to that.

She definitely hoped it didn't come to that, though. She hoped that she and Willy would hit it off and that she could develop the kind of relationship with him that Jace seemed to have. She hoped that, when Jace saw it, he would concede that a blood relative should have precedence over someone who was merely a designated guardian.

Clair towel-dried her hair, then fluffed and scrunched it with her fingers, thinking that gentle persuasion, finesse, tact, and diplomacy were most certainly the routes she wanted to take with Jace Brimley.

After meeting him, after seeing him, she knew that

he would not be an easy person to do battle with. Not with those big, bulging biceps and those broad, broad shoulders and those penetrating, blue eyes...

Clair paused in the middle of brushing a light dusting of blush on her cheeks and shook her head disgustedly at her own reflection. What was she thinking? That Jace Brimley would pummel her with those massive muscles or that lasers would shoot from his eyes to burn her alive?

Of course there was no physical danger from Jace Brimley. Any man who could so tenderly handle a toddler a fraction of his size was hardly likely to react with some kind of he-man, World Wrestling Federation antics when she finally admitted openly that she wanted to raise her nephew.

If he decided to fight her over Willy he would likely be a force to be reckoned with. But he wouldn't present any danger to her.

No, if she were honest with herself, she had to admit that what was really dangerous about Jace Brimley was the fact that her own thoughts kept wandering to things like his bulging biceps and broad shoulders and penetrating blue eyes. Not to mention the rest of his incredibly handsome face and well-built body and even the deep baritone of his voice...

Clair paused again, this time with her mascara wand halfway to her eye. She'd been so lost in thoughts of Jace Brimley that she hadn't even realized she'd moved on to eyeliner and mascara.

Oh, yes, there was definitely danger in her own wandering thoughts, she told herself as she finished her makeup and abandoned the small vanity table to go to the bedside to get dressed.

In essence, Jace Brimley was the enemy, and it certainly wasn't good strategy to think about the enemy in terms of staggering good looks and a spectacular body, she reasoned. Even if staggering good looks and a spectacular body were what the enemy had. It also wasn't good strategy to be distracted by the thrumming of her own heart every time he so much as flashed through her mind. That was truly where the danger lurked. And she wasn't going to allow any of it.

Of course, if she had met Jace Brimley at a party one Saturday night in Chicago, the staggering good looks and spectacular body and her own involuntary response to it all might make him someone she would be interested in personally.

But this wasn't a Saturday-night party in Chicago, and being interested in Jace Brimley personally was not part of the plan. She'd come to Elk Creek for one reason and for only one reason—to get her nephew—and that was all she was going to do here. Period.

But as she pulled on her socks and shoes, gave her hair a last fluff and applied a little lip gloss, she realized that the jitters she was feeling had an added element to them. An element that felt suspiciously like eagerness. And not just eagerness to see Willy again. Eagerness to get next door to see Jace Brimley again, too.

And no amount of willpower or reasoning with herself dispelled it.

Especially not when the image of the gloriously handsome man popped into her head again and her heart did another round of that uncontrollable thrumming in response.

I'm here for Willy. And for Kristin's sake, she reminded herself firmly. *And nothing else.*

But still her heart kept thrumming, and a little voice in the back of her mind said, *But if this was a Saturday-night party in Chicago things might be a whole lot different....*

Willy was on the porch when Clair crossed the two yards at exactly nine o'clock. He was so cute that just one look at him made her smile.

He had on miniature blue jeans with the legs cuffed on the bottoms to expose tiny suede work boots. He also wore the heavy parka Clair had seen on the sofa the night before. It wasn't zipped in front, so between the open sides she could see a navy-blue T-shirt with a bright picture of a cartoon dog and the words Scooby-Doo arched over the dog's head.

Clair wasn't sure what Willy was doing, but he was very busy scanning the perimeters of the porch, looking into the two empty clay flowerpots that sentried the front door and even studying the swing seat.

"Hi, Willy," she greeted as she reached the porch steps.

The little boy cast her a glance from beneath a suspicious frown but he didn't answer her. Instead he went on about his business.

Clair climbed the stairs and sat on the porch floor,

bracing her back against the railing so she could watch him at his own level.

"What are you doing?" she tried again.

"Nussin'," he finally responded under his breath, pressing his adorable red head as far as he could between the railing slats to peer into the surrounding bushes that hadn't yet begun to leaf.

"It doesn't look like you're doing nothing," Clair persisted, hoping she'd translated *nussin'* correctly. "Did you lose something?"

"No," he said forcefully, even though searching for something was what he appeared to be doing.

"Can I help?"

"No," he said, adding impatience and surliness to the forcefulness.

He must have spotted whatever he was hunting for because suddenly he ran as fast as his little legs would take him, around Clair, down the steps and toward the driveway where he snatched something from the side of the porch.

Then he bounded back the way he'd come and charged into the house as if Clair wasn't there at all.

"Whoa, boy!"

She heard Jace's deep voice come from just inside as she stood to follow Willy. By the time she was on her feet again Jace was out the door, one big hand on Willy's head to urge him in the same direction.

"'Mornin'," Jace said, ignoring Willy's obvious lack of desire to rejoin her.

"Good morning."

Willy tugged on Jace's pant leg—apparently a signal that he wanted to be picked up, because the tall man bent over and did just that, settling the child on one hip.

When he was situated, Willy whispered something in Jace's ear and in response to it, Jace said, "Her name is Clair. She's your aunt—that's someone like Josh and Beau and Ethan and Scott and Devon. They're your uncles, and ladies like them are called aunts."

Willy shook his head, vigorously, solemnly and muttered, "Ants're bugs."

Clair felt her heart clench at the continuing rejection, but she laughed at his reasoning, anyway.

"Some ants are bugs and other kinds of aunts are people. Clair is not a bug," Jace tutored. Then, in a confidential voice directed into the boy's ear, he added, "Why don't you say good morning to her?"

"No," Willy responded without hesitation and with as much force as his earlier nos to her.

"Come on. She's a nice lady. Pretty, too. And if I'm rememberin' right, she's come a long way to see you."

Willy shook his head once more, a stern refusal. Then he stuck his index finger in his mouth and glared at Clair.

"Okay," Jace conceded as if it were Willy's loss. "But me, I like pretty ladies."

Willy shook his head again and remained mute.

Jace ignored that, too, and focused his denim-blue eyes entirely on Clair. "He's had a lot of upheaval in the past few months," he said. "And he's two."

Clair nodded as if she understood, but she couldn't keep her spirits from deflating slightly at this second, less-than-enthusiastic beginning.

Then, in a cheerier tone, Jace said, "Shall we get goin'?"

"Sure," Clair agreed, putting some effort into hiding her disappointment that Willy wouldn't have anything to do with her.

To Willy, Jace said, "I see you found your tool belt. So we should be all set."

This time the small, bur-cut head bobbed up and down, and Willy held aloft the toy tool belt he'd located a few minutes earlier by the side of the porch.

Jace turned back to the house to close and lock the door. As he did, Clair's gaze went with a will of its own to the man himself.

He was dressed much like Willy was—cowboy boots instead of work boots, blue jeans, and a jean jacket over a faded red Henley shirt over a white crewneck T-shirt that showed beneath the Henley's open placket.

But it wasn't merely the clothes that Clair took notice of. It was also the way the clothes fit the man.

The T-shirt molded to impressive pectorals. The waist-length jean jacket was stretched to its limits by the breadth of his shoulders and the expanse of his muscular arms. And the jeans...oh, the jeans! They were just snug enough to cup a derriere to die for.

Clair's mouth went dry, her heart started thrumming all over again, and she felt as if her temperature had gone up.

Maybe she'd caught some kind of country fever, she thought. Some kind of country fever that was making her body react to things she shouldn't even be aware of.

Or maybe it was cowboy fever, she amended, none too patient with herself.

But country fever or cowboy fever, she forced her eyes off Jace's rear end in the nick of time as he spun back around on his heels with a sexy bit of grace and agility that made her think he was probably a good dancer.

He pointed his chin toward the black truck in the driveway and said, "Hope you don't mind sittin' in the middle. Willy's car seat has to be on the passenger's side because of the seat belt."

It wasn't sitting in the middle that she minded. The problem was the effect it would have on her to be that close to Jace.

"Maybe I should follow behind in my car," she suggested when it occurred to her, trying not to think about *his* behind....

"You can if you want but it seems silly. Unless you aren't plannin' to spend the whole day with us."

"No, it isn't that," she answered in a hurry, concerned that he'd gotten the impression she didn't want to be with Willy that long. "I just thought that if I was crowding you—"

"There's plenty of room," he assured her before she could finish her attempt to cover her tracks.

"Okay, then," she said much too happily, when the truth was that just the thought of being that near to

Jace on the truck's bench seat raised her temperature another notch. Cowboy fever. If there was such a thing, she really thought she had it.

But since there was no rectifying the situation, she went along with Jace and Willy to the truck, arriving on the driver's side at the same moment Jace did.

He reached in front of her and opened the door for her, then rounded the cab to deposit Willy in the car seat and buckle him in.

That was accomplished by the time Clair slid in next to the child. But her welcome there was cold as Willy frowned at her as if she were intruding, then presented her with the back of his head, looking through the side window in yet another rejection of her.

She really didn't know what to do about him. But before she could come up with anything, Jace was behind the wheel and she was left torn between the child who didn't want anything to do with her and the man whose very presence did too much to her.

And all she could do was hope that the trip they were about to embark on was short.

For a while, as Jace drove through town, neither of them said anything, and Clair was every bit as hypersensitive to his proximity as she'd feared she would be.

The scent of his woodsy, clean-smelling aftershave didn't help. In fact it almost seemed to intoxicate her and make her even more aware of every little detail about him. Even more vulnerable to what she thought had to be just plain animal magnetism.

He seemed to be trying to give her as much space as he could, because he was hugging the driver's side door, bracing his left elbow on the armrest and leaning his jawbone on his fist.

It was actually a pretty relaxed way to drive since he was using his right wrist to control the steering wheel on the straightaways, leaving his hand to dangle on the other side of the wheel.

But nothing could put more than an inch of distance between his thigh and hers, and Clair was excruciatingly aware of it. It left her with the inexplicable sense that she could feel the heat of that thigh seeping into her in a very sensual way....

"How far is this ranch you work on?" she asked, to escape her own reaction to him and in the hope that it wouldn't be long before they got to their destination.

Jace looked at her out of the corner of his eye and smiled as if he could take offense to that question but chose not to. "The ranch is about ten miles outside of town. But I'm not a hired hand. It's my family's place. My place. My dad passed away three years ago after a heart attack, but my brothers and my mother and I keep it going."

"Brothers—those would be the uncles you mentioned?"

"Right."

"I didn't count, but it sounded like there are a lot of them."

"Five."

"No sisters?"

"Nope. My dad always joked that my mom gave him sons because they couldn't afford ranch hands."

"So all six sons make their living on your family's ranch?"

"Everybody but my brother Devon. He's a veterinarian in Denver. The rest of us work the place, yeah, but we've all been known to pick up odd jobs here and there to supplement what the ranch brings in. My brother Josh, for instance, was just elected sheriff."

By then they were on the outskirts of Elk Creek, and Clair began to see what she assumed were ranches or farms—she couldn't tell the difference. Basically what she saw were huge stretches of open countryside with an occasional large house, barn or outbuilding sitting far back from the road.

Jace must have noticed her interest in the three houses they passed—all very impressive—because he said, "Our spread isn't up to par with what you're seein' so far. We're smaller."

There was a note to his voice that told her it was a sore spot with him.

"So you live in town and just go out to your ranch to work? Is there not a house on it?"

"Sure there's a house. I grew up in it, and my mother and brothers still live there. I just moved into town when I became Willy's guardian—that house belonged to Billy and Kim. Now, technically, it's Willy's. But I thought Willy had had enough trauma, and he didn't need to be moved out to the ranch on top of everything else."

"It must be inconvenient for you to live in Elk

Creek instead of on your land with your family, though.''

''Some, but it's no big deal. I may consider moving back with Willy later on, renting out the house in town. The money from something like that could pay for Willy's education when the time comes. Then, after he's all grown-up he can take the place over. But for now this is what's best for him.''

Clair glanced over at Willy. ''So you're already a homeowner, huh?'' she joked.

Willy looked at her as if she were speaking a foreign language and turned his head again.

''We're just up the road,'' Jace informed her as he turned off the main drag onto a flat dirt road that was a straight shot to a house that stood about a quarter of a mile ahead.

As they drew nearer Clair could see more details. The house was a two-story square box. A steep, black, shingled roof dropped eaves over three multipaned windows on the top level, and a matching roof shaded a wraparound porch on the lower level.

It was definitely not as fancy, as elaborate or as large as the houses they'd passed before, but it showed care in the flawless white paint and the black shutters that stood on either side of all the windows, including the two picture windows that looked out onto the porch.

There were homey, loving touches in the twin carriage lamps that adorned the shutters that bracketed the door, in the planters that hung in the center of each section of the cross-buck railing that surrounded the porch, and in the old-fashioned spindled benches and high-backed rocking chairs situated here and there.

But regardless of the care lavished on the place, it was still just an old farmhouse that couldn't compare to those other houses they'd driven by.

"Mop?" Willy said excitedly, as Jace drove around the house to the big red barn behind it.

"She's already gone by now, Willy. So's everybody else."

"Mop?" Clair repeated.

"That's what he calls my mother. Near as we can tell he heard all of us calling her Mom, figured she wasn't *his* mom, and settled for Mop."

"Mop," Willy said again in confirmation, as if it made perfect sense.

"We're getting a late start today or the whole gang would be here and I'd introduce you. As it is, there's no reason to go in when it's the paddock fence I'm fixin' today. But we have the run of the place if you need a bathroom or anything," he informed her as he pulled the truck to a stop near the barn's great door.

"I can keep Willy out of your way while you work," Clair suggested.

"I hep you, Unca Ace," Willy insisted, again with that two-year-old forcefulness, as if Clair were interfering.

"Uncle *Ace?*" she parroted, unable to suppress a laugh as she did.

"He doesn't do too well with *j*s," Jace explained, giving her a sheepish grin that was so charming and endearing she didn't have a doubt that it gave him tremendous leverage with whatever woman he used it on. Her included, although she didn't want to admit it.

Then, to Willy, he said, "Yep, you can help me. And maybe we'll put Clair to work, too."

Willy scowled at her but didn't come out with the usual no. That seemed to Clair like progress.

Jace got out of the truck, and Clair followed him, glancing around as he took Willy from the car seat.

Not that there was a lot to see—some farm equipment, a garage about the same size as the barn, with four doors and what looked to be an apartment on top. The winter's remaining bales of hay were stacked in a lean-to. Several towering apple trees provided shade for the rear of the house and the mud porch that jutted out from it. A brick-paved patio held a picnic table, benches and stacked lawn chairs awaiting summer.

"There you go, little man," Clair heard Jace say as he set Willy on his feet.

No sooner did he let go of the small boy than Willy took off like a shot for the barn, disappearing through the big open doors without a word to Jace.

"Where's he going?" Clair asked.

"To say good morning to Tom. He's our barn cat. Willy never gets near the barn without going in after him."

"Would you mind if I went, too?"

"No, go ahead. I need to get the wood out of the truck and start work. I'll be right over there." He nodded toward the white rail fence that surrounded an area of dirt beside the barn. The paddock, Clair assumed, although it didn't really matter to her what it was called.

Willy was all that was on her mind as she took off in the same direction he had, entertaining visions of the two of them bonding over the pet.

She expected to find boy and cat the moment she stepped through the barn's main door but all she saw was a long center aisle with empty stall after empty stall lining both sides.

"Willy?" she called.

The child didn't answer her, but from outside Jace's booming baritone said, "He'll be in the tack room."

Clair wasn't sure what a tack room was, but since there was a door at the end of the center aisle, she headed for that. Along the way she looked into each stall just in case, but to no avail. Neither Willy nor the cat were in any of them.

"Willy?" she called again tentatively as she approached the door.

She could see one end of a tall workbench. Harnesses, reins and various paraphernalia hung from hooks on the walls. But she still didn't see her nephew or the cat.

Until she actually reached the door.

But she'd only taken two steps in the direction of the workbench when the cat let out an angry meow, and Willy wailed, "Ouch!"

Then Willy scrambled out from under the workbench and charged passed her, crying loudly, "Unca Ace! Unca Ace!"

Terrified of what might be wrong, Clair ran after

him, arriving at Jace's side just as he scooped Willy into his arms.

"What'd you do, Willy?" he asked patiently, scanning a scratch on the boy's hand.

"I talked back of cat, cat talked back of me," Willy lamented.

"Mmm-hmm," Jace said as if he understood exactly what the little boy had said. "You were pulling Tom's tail again, weren't you? And he hissed at you, you told him to be quiet, and went right on pulling it until he scratched you. Right?"

"Yep," Willy said pitifully.

"You can't be mean to Tom. What did I tell you about that?"

"He's mean on me."

"He's only mean to you when you're mean to him first. You can't pull his tail."

"I wanna."

"Well, you can't. And if you do it again, I won't let you go in and see him anymore."

Out jutted Willy's bottom lip and down went his brows into a dark frown. But then he said, "I wanna hep you," in a conciliatory whine.

"You can help me as soon as we wash out that scratch."

And with that they took a quick, first-aid break in the mudroom.

Clair only watched from the sidelines because every time she got too near Willy insisted she, "Dit away!" as if she'd been the cause of his misery.

Then, once Jace was certain Willy was well taken care of, they all went back outside.

Jace had unloaded the new rails from the truck bed and stacked them on the ground behind it. He pointed at them as they passed them on their way back.

"You guys can bring those over to the fence," he suggested. "Willy can take one end and Clair can take the other."

It was clearly a chore he'd left purposely for them, because he could have hauled the whole lot of it in one trip himself. Clair appreciated that he was encouraging the togetherness so she could interact with her nephew. But Willy wanted no part of it, and the minute Clair put a hand on one of the rails, he dropped his end, picked up another board and dragged it himself.

"He's an independent little guy," Jace said apologetically when, after the third try, she'd given up and left the chore to Willy, settling near where Jace worked just to watch the boy.

"I suppose that's a good thing," Clair said. But she knew she didn't sound convincing.

Jace used the claw end of a hammer as leverage to pull off the damaged rails he intended to replace. He had a rhythm going, and it caught Clair's eye even as she meant to be only watching Willy.

But Jace was something to see as he braced a booted foot against the lowest rail, jammed the claw behind the board and nail and then put muscle into yanking them free.

Clair told herself not to pay attention to it. That

"Unca Ace" was not why she was there. But with the March sun streaking his hair with gold and illuminating his handsome face as perfectly as a photographer's lamp at a photo shoot, he was a hard sight to tear her gaze from.

When he'd pulled off a number of rails and Willy had all the new ones haphazardly deposited nearby, he said, "Okay, pal, if you're careful to grab the old boards in the middle where there aren't any nails you can take them to the trash for me. Maybe we can get Clair to stand over there and throw them in for us." Then, under his breath, he said to Clair, "He *has* to have help with that."

Willy might have needed her assistance, but that didn't mean he was interested in socializing during the process.

Clair followed him to a large metal trash receptacle where he gave each board to her as solemnly as if it were the Olympic torch. But she got no response to anything she said to him to try to draw him out, except when she asked about the picture on the front of his T-shirt. Then he said, "I watch Dooby-Doo on TV," and went back to ignoring her.

That was how the bulk of the day went, and by the end of it, Clair was both weary and dejected.

But she didn't want Jace to know it, and so, as they drove back into town, she decided to do some subtle pleading of her own case.

"It doesn't seem very practical to contend with a two-and-a-half-year-old while you work every day," she said, slightly out of the blue and confident that

Willy wouldn't be aware of the conversation because he'd fallen instantly asleep in his car seat.

He gave her the sideways glance he'd given her on their way out to the ranch, taking his eyes off the road for only a split second and not turning his head. "Oh, I don't know. I think we make a pretty good team."

"You must not get as much done, though. Stopping to deal with a child every few minutes is distracting, and the time it takes away from your work adds up."

Jace smiled mysteriously, and she had the impression that he was seeing through her again. "What are you, an efficiency expert?"

"I'm just saying that—"

"It isn't as if I'm in an office with a quota to fill. I don't see anything wrong with what we're doin'. If my job for the day can't be done with him around, one of my brothers is invariably doing something he can be there for, or my mother takes him with her to the McDermots' place. She works around their house, and they don't mind havin' Willy over if need be. One of their boys is a little older than he is, and they play real well together. Some days they ask for him to come."

Jace looked at her for a moment, somewhat pointedly, she thought. Then he said, "Seems to me this is a better way for a boy to grow up than havin' to spend his days indoors at a day care center or a baby-sitter's or something. He's out in the open, learnin' things, playin', gettin' his self assurance and self-esteem built up by findin' he can be a help and actually do some chores like he did today."

It was hard to disagree with any of that, because she'd seen all of what he was talking about, and he was right.

But she couldn't not argue her own side.

"There's something to be said for day care when they begin to work on skills kids need for school. Plus they learn there are rules they have to follow and they learn how to work and play with other kids. A good day-care center can give a child a head start."

"You think it's better for a boy to be shut up in an institution every day rather than be out in the fresh air and sunshine with somebody who's giving him one-on-one attention?"

"'Shut up in an institution'?" she repeated. "You make it sound like an insane asylum. There are playgrounds and equipment—it isn't as if kids are locked in windowless dungeons and fed gruel. They get accustomed to structure and order and schedules. They learn to compromise. They learn that there's a time for work and a time for play, that there needs to be a balance in life. They learn discipline and order. Hygiene and—"

Jace laughed. "Are you thinkin' Willy should be groomed for the military? Childhood as extended boot camp?"

"Of course not. It's just that there's something to be said for today's day-care centers and for being free to do your own work without the hindrance of a child."

The moment she said the word *hindrance* she knew

she'd made a mistake, and the sobering of Jace's expression only confirmed it.

Jace leaned forward enough to check on Willy, to make sure the little boy wasn't hearing any of this.

Then he said, "I haven't for a single minute thought of havin' Willy with me as a hindrance."

"I know. I didn't mean that the way it sounded. I just meant that there's nothing wrong with a child being cared for by someone other than a parent or guardian while the parent or guardian works."

"I enjoy havin' Willy with me. He enjoys bein' with me. I think we're both lucky to have the chance to spend this time together."

And that seemed to conclude the conversation as he pulled into his driveway.

Which was for the best as far as Clair was concerned, because she knew she'd lost more points than she'd gained all the way around today.

Jace got out of the truck and Clair followed him, stopping to wait near the hood while he went around to the passenger side to unbuckle Willy.

But as she stood there, she began to wonder where she should go from there. If she should continue to tag along into the house or if the end of the day signaled the end of her time with Willy and Jace—something she was suddenly inordinately loath to have happen.

She hated to invite herself to stay if Jace was tiring of her company, but she also didn't want to leave and have him think she'd had her fill, either.

Luckily Jace solved her dilemma.

"Tuesday night is pizza night at our house. Want to come back in an hour or so and see what an evening in the life of Willy Miller is like now that you've seen what his day involves?"

A swell of gratitude rose inside Clair, and it occurred to her that she liked this man very much. There was something so strong and confident about him that he wasn't threatened by the idea of sharing Willy—at least as things stood now. Strong and confident enough that he was trying to help her get to know her nephew, get closer to him, even if Willy wasn't cooperating.

It was just plain nice of him. And that was a refreshing change for her.

Not to mention that it made him all the more appealing....

"I'd like that," she said belatedly, when she realized she hadn't responded to his invitation yet.

"Great. An hour'll give me a chance to shower off some of today's grime and get my dough to risin'."

He could surprise her, too.

"Your dough? You mean you *make* the pizza?"

"Somebody always 'makes' the pizza, Clair," he said, teasing her by explaining the obvious.

"I know someone makes the pizza. I just didn't think, when you said it was pizza night, that you were the someone. I figured you ordered out."

"Can't order out pizza as good as I make."

"And you even make the dough?"

"Mmm-hmm. The sauce, too. I cook up a batch and can it myself."

"Amazing."

"I'm a man of many talents," he said with a voice full of innuendo and a lascivious arch to his eyebrow that made her laugh this time.

But she didn't doubt him. And she also realized that there was a part of her that was far too interested in learning just what all he *was* talented at....

"An hour then," she repeated. "I'd like to clean up, too. Can I bring something? I could run into town for—" She was going to say she could run into town for a bottle of wine but she realized that made it sound too much like they were planning a date. So she quickly changed course. "—for something for dessert. Does Willy like ice cream?"

"Sure, but there's some in the freezer if we get the urge. After my pizza you might not have room."

What Clair was afraid of was just what kind of urges she might end up having. But she didn't say that. Instead she played off the braggadocio in his last comment.

"Pretty proud of your pizza, are you?"

His supple mouth eased into a wicked grin, and only then did it occur to her that the way she'd said that had made it sound as if she was referring to something more personal than pizza. Something a whole lot more personal than pizza.

But he didn't miss a beat before saying, "Yeah, I am," in much the same tone.

Clair decided she'd better get away from there before either of them ventured any further into the flirting neither one should have been doing.

"I'll be back in an hour," she said with a hint of chastisement in her tone.

"I'll be here."

"See you in a little bit, Willy," she called to her nephew, who was hunkered down in serious study of a dead spider.

Willy ignored her yet again.

"Mind your manners, little man," Jace warned amiably enough.

"Bye-see-ya," the boy answered without looking away from the spider.

But Clair had successfully accomplished what she'd wanted, and whatever sparks had been flying between her and Jace were defused. Or at least they were muted some.

"I guess that says it all. Bye-see-ya," she parroted, heading off across the lawn toward Rennie Jennings's house.

But she could feel Jace's eyes on her as she did, and she only realized after she was doing it that she'd put the tiniest sway into her walk.

Knock it off, she ordered herself.

But even the command and the reminder that she wasn't there to start anything up with Jace didn't help. Her hips seemed to have a mind of their own, and they went right on swaying all the way inside.

Chapter Three

Clair climbed Jace's porch steps exactly one hour later. As she did she silently repeated to herself, *I'm here to see Willy. I'm here to see Willy. I'm here to see Willy.*

Not to spend the evening with Jace.

But she could hardly believe herself, knowing Willy would never notice that she'd showered and shampooed her hair for the second time today, reapplied blush, mascara and eyeliner, and carefully chosen her best cashmere turtleneck sweater to wear over her black slacks because the color made her skin look luminous.

She was there to see Willy. There to see Willy. There to see Willy...

"The door's open," Jace called from inside when she rang the bell.

Clair let herself in to Jace's second call. "We're in the kitchen." She followed the sound of his voice instructing Willy. "Pat it out like a mud pie the way I showed you."

From the living room she went into the dining room, then through the swinging door and into the kitchen, which she'd barely caught a glimpse of before. The walls were painted bright blue around the natural oak cupboards and white appliances. A large round table monopolized the center of the room, surrounded by four ladder-back chairs.

Jace was standing at the table, and Willy was beside him, kneeling on the seat of one of the chairs. There was a wooden pastry board in front of them both, and while Jace pressed dough into a round pizza pan at one end, Willy attempted to do the same with a considerably smaller piece on a cookie sheet at the other end of it.

"Hi," Jace greeted her, glancing up from what he was doing to cast her a welcoming smile that seemed to make the kitchen even brighter.

"Hi," Clair answered. Then she added, "Hi, Willy."

Willy, of course, barely muttered a "Hi" in return, without so much as looking at her.

"He's learnin' to be a pizza man," Jace said proudly.

"Pizza man," the little boy repeated as if it were a title he was eager to have.

Clair watched the two of them pressing floured fingers into the soft dough to spread it ever wider. Willy put too much pressure into it most of the time and jammed his fingers all the way through, leaving holes here and there.

But Jace was more adept, and she marveled at how such powerful hands could be so agile. Agile enough, she supposed, to knead a woman's flesh much the same way, with just the right amount of pressure, just the right amount of tenderness, just the right amount of firmness...

"Pull up a seat," he said, interrupting her wandering thoughts none too soon. "We're just about to put on all the trimmings."

Clair straightened her posture, took a deep breath and once more reminded herself that she was only there to see Willy.

"Can I do something to help?" she asked.

"Pour yourself a glass of wine."

So she hadn't been the only one with that idea.

"There are three glasses near the bottle on the counter," Jace said with a nod in the direction of the tiled countertop near the sink.

"Willy gets wine?"

Jace made a face at her. "He gets the grape juice next to it. But if you don't put it in a wineglass he'll only want what we're having."

"Oh," Clair said, chagrined at overlooking the obvious.

She did the honors, surprised to find the wine he had breathing on the counter was a particularly good vintage.

He really was more than he appeared to be on the

surface, she thought. Or maybe she was overlooking the obvious when it came to him, too.

She supposed it was easy enough to do. There he was, a big, rugged cowboy with an extremely handsome face and an amazing body, dressed pretty much the same each time she'd seen him—in blue jeans and, tonight, a plain tan-colored shirt.

It was difficult to look past those superficial things, and the stereotype that came with them, to think that he might be a chef who made his own pizza dough and canned his own sauce. Or that he might have the same kind of knowledge about wines that the last man she'd been involved with had after taking classes on the subject to impress his friends. Or that Jace would be as talented as he was with a small child.

But there it all was, making him a more interesting person than she had expected him to be. A more interesting person than she *wanted* him to be, because it made it so much harder not to be intrigued. And impressed. And affected by him.

When she had the wine and grape juice poured, she took the glasses to the table.

Jace and Willy were both spreading thick tomato sauce on their respective crusts. Willy kept an eagle eye on Jace's every movement, mimicking him as best he could but still slopping some of the sauce over the edges of the dough, while Jace managed to spread an even layer, leaving just the right amount of plain crust around the perimeter.

On went pieces of fresh mozzarella, then sliced black olives. But Willy stopped there while Jace added roasted peppers, onions, fresh mushrooms and sausage to the main pie.

Willy occupied himself by putting olive rings on each of his fingers.

"Lookit," he said to Jace, giggling at his innovation.

Jace laughed at him but said, "Don't put those back in the bowl now."

Willy didn't. He ate each one off his fingers.

Then the pizzas went into the oven, and the two of them cleared the mess with Clair looking on.

"Have you ever thought of being a teacher?" she asked Jace when he dispatched Willy to set the table and the tiny child actually did it, apparently having been taught how before tonight.

"Now you want to coop *me* up in a building every day?" Jace joked, referring to their day care discussion on the drive home earlier.

"You're pretty incredible with kids."

He shrugged negligently as he put a salad together. "It doesn't take more than a little time and patience. And likin' 'em."

"And you *do* like them, don't you?"

"Yep. Maybe it comes from being the firstborn. My mom always said she taught me to walk and talk and I took over from there with all my brothers so she didn't have to. Mainly I remember just wantin' 'em to talk instead of cry all the time and to be able to get around on their own so we could play."

"I was the oldest child, too. Well, obviously, since you knew Kristin, you knew *she* wasn't the oldest. I think it always made me feel sort of parental toward her.''

Clair wasn't sure why she'd told him that but she did know that she hadn't meant to allow sadness in her voice. Yet it was there, anyway, and in response Jace seemed to sober some.

''There was just you and Kristin? No other brothers or sisters?'' he asked as if he were genuinely interested.

''No, just us. I know it seems like there should have been some other kids between us—nearly ten years is quite an age span. But there weren't any.''

''Be kind of hard not to mother a sister that much younger.''

''Mmm. Especially when there wasn't a real mother in the picture.''

His eyebrows rose slightly. ''I didn't know that. Kristin didn't talk much about her family. She just said that she'd shamed them and so she couldn't have anything to do with them anymore.''

''Oh, that's not true!'' Clair lamented in pure reflex to the stab that statement unintentionally delivered.

The timer went off just then to let them know Willy's pizza was finished baking.

Jace took it out of the oven, protecting his hands with only a dish towel.

''This has to cool until the other pizza's done,'' he told Willy, who was eager to dig into his masterpiece.

Then Jace began to dress the salad and returned to the conversation with Clair. ''I didn't mean to upset you. I was just repeatin' what Kristin told Kim and

Billy. We all assumed from what she said that her family had turned their backs on her."

"I don't know, maybe it seemed that way to her," Clair said. "But it shouldn't have. Not really. I had taken kind of a hard line with her, but—"

"You don't have to explain. I know how problems can develop in families. There's one in mine."

"But that's just it, there wasn't a real problem. As far as I knew, anyway. There was just…I don't know, a bump in the road that she didn't let me have a clear understanding of."

"A communication problem," Jace surmised.

"I don't even think you could call it that. Until the last time I saw her, she and I were as close as two sisters could be. We shared everything. There was no competition between us. I considered her my best friend and I thought she considered me hers. Of course, the same could hardly be said about Kristin and Dad…."

The timer rang again, signaling that the main pizza was finished. While Jace repeated the process he'd followed for Willy's pie—raising the crust with a knife to make sure it was browned on bottom and taking it out of the oven to serve—Clair considered just how far she should go in detailing her family's shortcomings.

But as she did, it occurred to her that if she gave Jace some background information he might begin to get a clearer picture of where she was coming from and what had transpired three years ago. And even though it was private and personal, leaving him with the image Kristin had apparently given certainly couldn't aid her cause in gaining custody of Willy.

So once she, Jace and Willy had full plates and were settled down to eat, she said, "Our mother died in a car accident when Kristin was six months old. That left my dad alone with us and, well, he wasn't... isn't...a great father. I love him, don't get me wrong. But it's hard for him to think of anyone but himself, and he has sort of a chip on his shoulder. He also isn't the most reliable person in the world. Even before my mom died he changed jobs at the drop of a hat, always because someone wasn't recognizing his potential or was slighting him or for some other reason that was usually more in his own skewed perception of things than in reality."

"Kristin never said anything about her mother, but she made a comment here and there about her father. She didn't have much good to say about him."

"My mother's death didn't improve him by any means. In fact, without her steadying influence he started not only changing jobs but moving Kristin and me around from state to state every time, too. And he got married—and divorced—three more times. It didn't make for a very stable or warm or loving home environment. I got out as soon as I could, which meant going away to college."

Clair paused long enough to tell him how delicious the pizza was.

"What'd I tell you?" he said as if the compliment were his due. But she could tell he was pleased that she liked it.

Then she went on. "After college I landed a good job at an advertising agency in Chicago—the same one I'm with now, as a matter of fact. I started as a copy writer and I made enough money to get my own apartment not far from where Dad and Kristin were living. I was determined to provide a stable life for myself and a place where Kristin could come and stay when she needed a refuge."

"You didn't want her to move in with you full-time?" Jace asked, sounding curious but not judgmental.

"I did. And she wanted to. But Dad took that as a huge affront and threw a fit. So instead Kristin would just say we were having a girls' night or a sleep-over at my place and stay four or five nights a week."

"And your father took that all right?"

"I told you, he's a very self-involved person. It was the idea of Kristin actually moving to my place that he thought made him look like a bad father. But doing it the way we did just gave him more free time to pursue whatever woman he was after at the moment. And he liked that."

"Four or five nights a week should have been pretty good for her, though," Jace allowed.

"I thought it was. She said it was. Things seemed better than they had been in a long, long while. But then three months before she was ready to graduate from high school she came to me insisting that she was dropping out of school."

"I wouldn't have stood for that," Jace said definitively as he helped Willy have a slice of the larger pizza since the child decided the one he'd made wasn't as good.

"Kristin wouldn't tell me anything concrete about why she wanted to drop out—not that I would have been in favor of it, anyway—but all she would say was that her boyfriend had dumped her and she'd had an argument with her friends. I thought that was perfectly normal teenage stuff that would blow over, and I told her so. But that it was absolutely not a reason to drop out of school."

"I agree."

"Well, she didn't. She dug in her heels and said she was not going back to school no matter what. We went round and round about it but she just wouldn't budge, and so I finally said that I couldn't support her decision and that I wouldn't be her sanctuary in that case, either. I told her I'd do whatever I could to help her get through the last few months till graduation, that I'd even go to bat with Dad or make up some reason why she had to stay with me all the time until she was finished with the year but that if she dropped out she was totally on her own."

"And you were hoping that would scare her out of the idea."

"Absolutely," Clair said. "That was my only goal."

But the memory of that last time she'd seen her sister was so hard for her that it formed a lump in her throat and she couldn't go on eating. She could barely talk.

"But Kristin dropped out, anyway," Jace guessed,

prompting her but also, it seemed, trying to help her through the sudden rough patch she'd hit.

Clair shrugged helplessly. "She just disappeared. That night—the night I gave her the ultimatum—after I went to bed, she slipped out of the apartment, and that was the last I ever saw of her or heard from her."

Clair took a sip of wine in hopes that it might help her fight the tears that welled up in her eyes. She'd cried often enough over this; she didn't want to do it again in front of Jace and Willy.

When she finally gained some control she said, "Kristin didn't tell me—she didn't even hint—that she was pregnant. I didn't have any idea until the Millers' lawyer contacted us about Willy."

"Wow."

"Of course I realized then what had been going on with her. She must have been too embarrassed to think about going back to school. Too embarrassed to even let me know what was really going on. But…"

Clair had to stop and try to get hold of herself again or she really was going to break down. And she *so* didn't want to. Bearing the burden of the shame she felt for what had happened with Kristin was bad enough; she didn't want to lay it out for Jace to see. She didn't want to do anything that might make him feel sorry for her, because she honestly didn't believe she deserved sympathy. Not after the way things had ended up because of her actions.

Only when she thought she could continue in a normal voice did she say, "Kristin's boyfriend—I assume the father of the baby—had dumped her for someone else, and he was being brutal about the fact that he didn't want anything more to do with her. When I found out she had been pregnant I put two and two together. I'm sure facing him with the news, or even going back to school and having one of her friends let the word get out, was more than she could stand. And of course she had to know how my father would have reacted—an unwed teenage daughter was definitely not something he would have been nice about. But she could have told me. I would have stood by her no matter what and we could have worked things out together.''

''But she didn't give you the chance.''

''I'm not making excuses for myself.''

''I didn't think you were. I don't see where there are any excuses that need to be made. You did the right thing based on the information you had at the time. It was Kristin's choice to take off without telling you the truth.''

''But if I hadn't given her an ultimatum maybe she would have eventually told me. Or if I'd listened more closely or been more open or more patient or—''

''Stop,'' he commanded in a quiet, kind, gentle tone. His blue eyes looked directly into hers and somehow forced her to focus outside herself, outside the memories she'd been torturing herself with, outside her own guilt and pain.

''You didn't do anything wrong,'' he told her. ''Do you hear me? You did the best you could have done for your sister before that night, and that night you did the best thing for her under the circumstances as you knew them. You're not to blame for anything.''

''Except because of what happened that night I lost touch with my sister, she ended up dying alone in an apartment she might not have been in otherwise, and now you're raising my nephew instead of his mother or even me.''

Jace shook his head. ''Things happen the way they're supposed to, Clair. I don't know why. You don't know why. But what I do know is that anything that takes as crazy a route as this whole thing has taken was meant to be.''

''What was meant to be was that you should end up raising Willy?''

''Maybe. And maybe, too, what was meant to be was that, for whatever reason, our paths would cross.''

He was still holding her eyes with his, and that statement given at another moment might have been very romantic. But that wasn't how he'd delivered it. He'd said it matter-of-factly and without any insinuation or innuendo or flirting or lasciviousness. He was only trying to comfort her.

Yet on the heels of that innocent comfort Clair suddenly flashed on the image of him comforting her with more than just words. She flashed on the image of him comforting her with those big, hard arms around her. With kisses that would be sweet and tender. And then maybe not so sweet and tender. Maybe passionate.

She realized belatedly where her mind had wandered and yanked it back into line.

What's wrong with me? she thought. How, even in

the midst of thinking about the worst things she'd been feeling since learning about Kristin and the baby, could she slip into thoughts of Jace Brimley holding her, kissing her?

Maybe it was just gratitude, she told herself, since no one before him had told her she wasn't at fault for what had happened to her sister, to her nephew. And, in fact, her father had been the first to lay blame at her doorstep.

Yes, gratitude. That's all there was to it....

"Done now," Willy announced out of the blue then, oblivious to what was going on around him. Oblivious to Clair's heightened emotional state—both the one over her sister or the one she'd just worked herself into over Jace.

Jace broke off their eye contact then, and only when he did, did Clair realize he'd been held in her gaze, too. And she wondered what had been going through his mind when kissing had been going through hers?

But whatever spell had been mesmerizing them was broken and so was the subject of Kristin and the past, as Willy demanded attention.

"We've been neglecting you, haven't we?" Clair said to him as she worked her way out of whatever it was that had just woven itself around her and Jace.

It seemed to take him a split second longer than it had taken her to come back to the moment, and when he did his voice was slightly deeper, more husky. "Why don't you go get ready for your bath, Willy," he suggested. "Get your towel and whatever toys you want to bring in tonight."

Willy's chubby-cheeked face once more pinched into a frown, and he pointed a stubby index finger at Clair while addressing Jace. "Her no see me."

Maybe his modesty shouldn't have been amusing but something about the way he'd said that made both Clair and Jace smile. It also eased the tension, the electric charge in the air between them.

"Okay, Clair doesn't have to come in if you don't want her to. But I promised she could hear your bedtime story afterward and we can't go back on a promise."

He'd made no such promise to her, but Clair was grateful that he was attempting to include her before Willy could order her out of that portion of the nightly ritual, too.

"Why don't I just put the dishes in the dishwasher while I wait," she said.

"Company doesn't do the dishes," Jace decreed.

"Okay," Clair pretended to agree. Then she waited for Jace and Willy to leave her alone to do them, anyway.

The bath and the kitchen cleanup took about the same amount of time, because just as Clair was rinsing out the sink a sullen, begrudging little voice from behind her said, "You could come now."

She turned to find Willy in footed pajamas decorated with the same cartoon dog that had been on his shirt.

"More Scooby-Doo, huh?" she commented as Willy led her out of the kitchen, up the stairs and to a bedroom decorated with a bear and train motif.

"Dooby-Doo," Willy yelled like a war cry just before running and jumping onto a small twin bed.

As Jace pulled a rocking chair from a corner to the bedside he said, "How 'bout you sit in Clair's lap tonight while I read?"

"No," was Willy's resounding answer. "You lap."

Jace gave Clair an apologetic shrug and sat in the rocker himself. "Why don't you sit on the bed," he offered as a consolation prize as Willy wasted no time climbing into his lap and settling in, complete with what looked to be a washcloth that he poked a finger into and began stroking his own cheek with.

Clair did as Jace had suggested and sat on the edge of the bed.

She ached to have Willy respond to her the way he did to Jace. To have the toddler climb into her lap. To have him snuggle against her as the end-of-the-day weariness overtook him and the ball of energy he'd been since morning turned into a soft, cuddling little sweetheart.

But if she couldn't have that just yet, the next best thing was seeing him that way with Jace.

The small boy curled into the cocoon of the big man's body as Jace read rhyming, sing-song words in a hushed baritone, his huge hands dwarfing the child's book he held.

It was a picture for a family album. A picture to pull out years and years down the road to tug at heartstrings and recall that there weren't only special occasions that were momentous, that some small moments were pretty special, too.

Willy fell asleep before Jace was halfway through the book, but Clair didn't tell him. She just went on enjoying the sight of the sleeping child and of the man who held him.

She couldn't help marveling again at Jace Brimley. At all the parts of which he was made. The incredible-to-look-at physical parts and the inner parts, too. And even though she might not know him well yet, she already had no doubt that he was something pretty terrific.

When he'd finished the book, he glanced down at his charge. Finding Willy sleeping made him smile the softest smile Clair had ever seen from a man.

Then he raised his glance to her and bathed her in that same smile.

He motioned for her to get up with just a tilting of his head and then he set the book on the nightstand and very carefully eased Willy from his lap into bed.

Once he had the boy situated, he tucked the covers around him, switched on a horse-shaped night-light and turned off the lamp.

Clair watched him press a kiss to the boy's fore-head, and then he turned to her, pointing toward the door as he placed a hand at the small of her back to guide her out of the room.

That hand at the base of her spine, through her clothes, was nothing more than a gentlemanly gesture. But it sent tiny lightning bolts from that spot all the way through her.

He had a magic touch with Willy, she thought, and maybe it extended to her, too.

But his hand only stayed on her back as they left the room, and Clair felt an unexpected wave of disappointment at the loss when he removed it. Enough of a wave of disappointment to warn her that with Willy not awake to chaperone them she was in dangerous territory.

"It's been a long day. I should get going," she said before her willpower failed her and she gave in to the temptation to linger.

Jace didn't argue as they headed away from the bedrooms toward the stairs. He just said, "Willy has a doctor's appointment tomorrow—a recheck on an ear infection—so we won't go out to the ranch. I told him we'd go to the park afterward as a treat. You're welcome to come."

Was she honestly hearing a note of hopefulness in his tone?

She couldn't be sure. But one way or another she did feel perfectly welcome. She just wasn't sure to what.

"To the doctor's appointment or to the park?" she asked to clarify.

"Both. Although I have to warn you he won't behave too well at the doctor's appointment."

"That's okay, I'd like to tag along again. I keep hoping that the more time I spend around him the more he'll get used to me and maybe eventually warm up."

"I'm sure he will."

They went down the stairs side by side and, with the front door in sight, Clair said, "I really appreciate everything you did today and tonight to try to get him interested in me. Even if it didn't work.''

''Sure.''

When they reached the entrance to the house, Clair put one hand on the knob, but rather than turning it to open the door she paused to look up at Jace.

He was studying her very intently, and she wasn't sure why.

''Do I have something on my face?'' she joked, feeling her nose, chin and one cheek just in case.

He smiled again. A smile different from that tender one earlier. A purely adult smile full of charm and deviltry and a simmering sensuality.

''I was just thinkin' how much you look like Willy around the eyes. Yours sparkle the same way his do. And around the mouth, too...''

He was staring openly at her mouth. But then, she was staring openly at his, too, as those earlier thoughts of kissing rushed back into her mind.

''It's the Fletcher mouth,'' she said for no good reason and in a voice that was far too breathy, too sexy, too inviting.

''Is that so?'' he nearly whispered back much the same way.

And then he was leaning forward. Very slowly. Until he touched his lips to hers.

But only for the briefest of moments before he straightened up and away from her.

''I probably shouldn't have done that, huh?'' he said, but the upward curve of just one corner of his mouth belied any regret.

"Probably not," she agreed but without enough force to be convincing.

Yet even as she recognized a longing in her for another kiss, for a better one, for one more like those she'd fantasized about, she knew this really wasn't something they should be doing. Not when she'd come there to take Willy away from him if she could.

So she turned the knob she was still holding and finally opened the front door.

"What time is the doctor's appointment tomorrow?" she asked, forcing a less personal tone into her voice.

"One. We'll leave about twelve forty-five."

"Okay. I'll be here."

"So will we," he joked feebly.

"Thanks for dinner. It really was great pizza."

He nodded, but he was still staring at her, and the compliment didn't seem to matter as much now as it had when they were at the table.

"I'll see you guys tomorrow," she added.

Again he only nodded, as if he were lost in thought. Thought that centered on her.

"Good night," she said.

"'Night."

He took a step nearer and raised a hand to the door's edge above her, bringing him near enough that for a moment Clair thought he might be going to kiss her again.

Or maybe it was just wishful thinking.

But he didn't. Instead he opened the door wider for her, and Clair took that as her cue to actually leave.

So she muttered a second good-night and did just that.

But as she walked across the lawns back to Rennie Jennings's house, she could still feel Jace's lips against hers, as if even that oh-so-quick kiss was enough to leave an imprint on her.

An imprint that allowed her to keep the memory of his mouth on hers clear and crisp.

So she could take it with her all the way to bed.

And relive it.

Whether it was wise or not....

Chapter Four

Clair's hostess, Rennie Jennings, managed the church her brother ministered to. But, by coincidence, she wasn't working the next morning, and since Clair wasn't scheduled to go over to Jace's house until twelve forty-five, Rennie suggested that she and Clair have a big country breakfast together and use the time to get to know each other.

Rennie wasn't kidding when she said a *big* country breakfast. Pancakes, scrambled eggs, bacon, sausages, hash-brown potatoes, a fresh fruit cocktail with yogurt, juice and coffee. There seemed to Clair to be enough food for ten people when the two of them sat down at Rennie's kitchen table to eat.

But it wasn't the food she was interested in.

Sharing the leisurely meal gave Clair the opportunity to do something she'd been wanting to do since arriving in Elk Creek—ask questions about Jace.

Which was exactly what she did as soon as she found a lull in the exchange of getting-to-know-each-other information about herself and Rennie.

"So, have you known Jace Brimley long?" was how she launched into it as she had her second cup of coffee and pushed her plate away.

If Rennie found anything suspicious in the change of subject, she didn't show it.

"Not long, no. Only since I moved to town six months ago. But you don't have anything to worry about when it comes to Jace—if you're wondering about him raising your nephew."

Rennie already knew the family connection by the time Clair had appeared at her door the first night.

"Jace is a great guy," her hostess assured her. "You won't find a better man."

"I'm not looking for a man," Clair said much too quickly, much too defensively.

"For raising Willy," Rennie clarified, but there was a sly note in her voice that prompted Clair into more self-defense.

"Well, yes, for raising Willy. But I'm not in the market for any kind of personal or romantic relationship with Jace or any other man right now." The only thing she was in the market for, she tried to convince herself, was finding out if he had a flaw she hadn't spotted yet. A flaw that she might be able to use to persuade a judge that it would be better for her to raise Willy, if it came down to a judge making that decision.

"I'm just curious about the type of person he is," Clair insisted.

Rennie, who was a girl-next-door type of pretty, smiled a gleaming smile that said she still didn't believe Clair was as objective about Jace as Clair insisted she was. But she played along, anyway.

"Let's see, the kind of person Jace Brimley is," she said, as if her answer required some thought. "Well, for starters, I can tell you what Billy and Kim Miller said about him during the brief time I knew them before their accident—when they were trying to fix me up with him."

"They tried to fix you up with him?"

"Sure. A single woman moves into town, meets her neighbors who have a single male friend of about the same age—getting them together is the first thing they think about."

Clair worked at ignoring the unpleasant feelings that arose in her and instead tried to keep things on track. "Okay, tell me what kind of person they said he was."

"They said he was the kind of person who was always there for them—helping Billy move heavy furniture when he needed to, helping him work on his car. Kim told me it was Jace they put as a reference when they were applying for Willy's adoption. And then, of course, he stepped in when his friends were killed to raise their son—that says a lot about him. And he did it generously, selflessly and without a thought as to how it might inhibit his social life, to suddenly become a daddy by default."

There was certainly nothing there that wasn't admirable.

"What about what you know about him yourself, firsthand?" Clair persisted nonetheless.

"Well, when I first moved in I needed some plumbing repairs done, and Kim said Jace could do them for me. So I hired him. He did everything I needed him to do, and then, when he found out I needed more done than I could afford, he did the rest, too. Without charging me one extra cent."

"He worked here?" Clair repeated, stuck on that portion of what Rennie had said and barely hearing the rest. "So the two of you must have spent a lot of time together. Alone." And the image of that only made those unpleasant feelings she was trying to ignore grow. Unpleasant feelings that seemed suspiciously like jealousy.

"Yeah, between his working around here and moving in next door after the accident, I'd say that I've gotten to know Jace pretty well—well enough to know that he's also the kind of person who shovels my walks and the walks of Mrs. Branch, the elderly woman who lives on the other side of him, when it snows, without being asked. He calls Mrs. Branch every other day, too, to check on her and ask if she needs anything. He runs her errands if she can't find anyone else to help her out. And," Rennie added as the coup de grâce, "he also has some of the best buns in town."

That last part caught Clair by surprise and made her laugh.

"Is that something the minister's sister is supposed to notice, let alone say?"

"How can I help but notice, and what's wrong with saying it?" the irreverent Rennie answered.

"Could it be you who's doing a little man shopping?" Clair said, turning the tables on her hostess and wanting her own curiosity satisfied once and for all about what might or might not be between Rennie and the handsome man next door.

"I suppose it sounds as if I'm the president of Jace's fan club, but I'm not," Rennie assured her so easily it had to be true. "Actually, I've kind of marveled at the fact that I'm not attracted to him. I mean, I like him, he's a stand-up guy and one of the most gorgeous accumulations of human flesh I've ever seen. I enjoy talking to him. I'm always glad for his help. But beyond that—zilch. Nada. No pitter-patter of my heart when I catch sight of him. No rushing of blood through my veins at the sound of his voice. No stars in my eyes when he crosses my mind. Nothing. No man-woman chemistry at all."

Relief washed through Clair so thoroughly that she almost deflated in her chair. It wasn't a good sign, and she knew it. It meant that it would have mattered if Rennie had said she was head-over-heels in love with Jace, and it shouldn't have.

And as if that fact wasn't alarming enough, Clair was also not happy to realize that everything Rennie had just said *didn't* happen to her with Jace, *did* happen to Clair.

But she tried not to think about it and instead, once more, yanked her focus back to her real purpose.

"So I guess he's just perfect?" she said dubiously.

"Were you looking for imperfections?" Rennie countered.

"No," Clair lied in a hurry. "It's just that he seems too good to be true."

"Oh, I wouldn't say that. I'm sure he leaves his dirty socks lying around or snores or picks his teeth at the table or *something*. But when it comes to character flaws, I haven't seen any evidence of them."

Which certainly wouldn't help in any kind of custody battle.

On the other hand, it was reassuring to know that she wasn't overlooking something. To know just what her competition's strengths were. To know what she was up against.

And, oh, boy, did she want to be up against him! Literally....

But that was an imperfection in *her*. An imperfection she needed to conquer.

She'd told Rennie that she wasn't interested in any kind of personal or romantic relationship with Jace, and she'd meant it. No matter who he was or how great or how incredible looking.

They had opposing goals, and she had better not forget it.

"Well, I'm glad to know that he's a decent man," Clair said.

But no matter how decent a man Jace was, her

sights were set on only one male—Willy—and that was all there was to it.

So, thinking about Jace in terms of any personal or romantic relationship was out of bounds.

As out of bounds as kissing him had been....

But what was past was past and there was nothing she could do about that now. She could only work harder to curb her thoughts in the future and make sure that, under no circumstances whatsoever, did she *kiss* him again.

The problem was that, as she and Rennie started to clean their breakfast mess and returned to inconsequential chitchat, in the back of her mind Clair was reliving yet again that courtly little kiss Jace had bestowed the night before.

And to make matters worse, she was also counting how much longer it was till twelve forty-five when she got to see him again....

"No dot-or. Did it lasterday."

"Yes, doctor. And you didn't see him yesterday, you saw him ten days ago."

Clair, Jace and Willy were in Jace's truck again, on their way to Willy's doctor's appointment. Willy wasn't happy about it, and his chubby-cheeked little face was pinched into a scowl. Certainly he hadn't been thrilled to have Clair added to the mix when she'd arrived just as Jace was putting him in his car seat.

"No dot-or," the toddler repeated.

"I told you, we have to have your ears checked to

make sure the infection went away,'' Jace explained calmly. ''It won't take long, it won't hurt, and if you're a good boy we'll go to the park afterward.''

Clair was sitting in the center of the bench seat just as she had the day before on their way to and from Jace's family's ranch. Even though she'd been careful to keep as much distance between herself and Jace as she could, hearing the promise of a trip to the park spurred her to lean slightly toward him to say under her breath, ''Isn't bribery bad form?''

He gave her a sideways glance and a crooked smile. ''I like to think of it as a reward.''

The doctor's office was on the ground floor of a three-story redbrick building that faced the town square. It looked like an old mansion, and when Clair mentioned that Jace confirmed it. It was the Molner Mansion, he informed her, donated to Elk Creek by one of the town's original founders and turned into a medical facility complete with doctor's office, dentist's office, a small out-patient surgical suite and a few hospital rooms that were only used in emergencies.

Jace parked in a lot adjacent to the building, and as Clair climbed down from the truck, he took Willy out of the car seat. But Willy was still not inclined to go willingly and had a mini sit-in right there on the tarmac. Jace merely bent over, picked him up and carried him in.

''No dot-or!'' Willy was protesting once more as they went inside, and Clair was glad to see there weren't any other patients in the waiting room.

A nurse stood behind the reception desk, but she seemed to take no notice of the little boy's tantrum and merely showed them to an examining room, assuring them that the doctor would be in directly.

She was right. She'd barely closed the door behind herself before the doctor opened it to join them.

The doctor, Jace had explained on the way, was a man named Bax McDermot. Bax McDermot had only recently moved to town to be with the rest of the large McDermot clan—the family Jace's mother worked for.

But Clair didn't see any signs of social snobbery when the doctor entered the examining room. He and Jace were on a first-name basis as they shook hands like two old friends and exchanged some sports talk before Jace introduced her. The doctor greeted her warmly, too, and then tried to get down to business with Willy.

It was easier said than done.

Jace was beside the examining table where Willy stood leaning against him. But the moment the doctor's attention was focused on Willy he turned his back to him, clamped his arms around Jace's neck and climbed the big cowboy's body enough to hide his face behind Jace's neck.

"We have to take a look in those ears, Will," Bax McDermot said.

"No!" came the muffled reply from behind Jace's head.

To Clair, even just looking on, this was very embarrassing. Willy's negative reaction to her was one thing, but to act like that in a doctor's office was something else. And she didn't have the foggiest idea how it should be handled.

Jace, on the other hand, seemed to take it in stride. He didn't lose his temper, didn't raise his voice, didn't even seem uncomfortable with the display of two-year-old defiance. He also didn't cajole or wheedle or beg the boy to behave—which Clair was inclined to do. Instead he was as relaxed as usual, kindly but firmly maneuvering Willy so that the doctor could look in his ears, coaching and assuring the child along the way until Bax McDermot pronounced Willy's infection completely gone.

And once again Clair was impressed by Jace.

But it also occurred to her that maybe the time she'd allotted to try to win Willy over could have a second use, too. Maybe she could also use it to learn from Jace. He was so adept with the boy that every minute with them could be an instruction in parenting if she paid close attention.

Well, she was paying close attention—just not to Jace's parenting technique. She was paying more attention to the way his jeans rode his hips and hugged that great rear end Rennie had remarked about earlier. More attention to the way his broad shoulders and muscular chest filled out the crisp beige Western shirt he wore.

But from that moment on, she vowed she was going to concentrate instead on how Jace dealt with Willy, so that if she did get to raise her nephew she would know what to do in difficult situations like the one in the doctor's office. She obviously had a lot to learn and she couldn't think of a better teacher than Jace.

If only she could keep her wandering thoughts in line....

Even though Willy hadn't been particularly good, after the appointment Jace led the way to the play park. It was within walking distance of the medical building, and Clair refrained from pointing out that it hadn't worked as a bribe and that, instead, Jace was rewarding Willy's lack of cooperation.

But pointing that out might have caused Jace to cancel, and the end of the outing could well have ended her time with the two of them. And that wasn't what she wanted at all.

So she kept quiet and just went along.

The play park was actually the school playground, too, but since there were other preschool children there it clearly served the whole community.

With the ordeal of the doctor's visit behind him, Willy was his old self again and, as soon as they got near enough for him to safely be let loose, he ran on stubby legs to the swings, hollering for his "Unca Ace" to push him "reary, reary, high."

"Go ahead," Jace urged Clair. "Why don't you do it?"

Yet again she appreciated his generosity in stepping aside to allow her something that might cause her nephew to like her better.

But still Willy was not receptive. He complained that she didn't push him high enough and wanted his

"Unca Ace" to do it. So after a few pushes she stepped aside and returned the honors to Jace.

That was pretty much how the afternoon went as Clair continued the struggle to make headway with Willy. The small boy still preferred Jace when it came to helping him climb the slide's ladder and the rungs on the monkey bars. He still preferred Jace when it came to the seesaw. And it was still only Jace he wanted with him in the sandbox.

At the end of the day they had a fast-food dinner at a drive-in hamburger joint, and Clair did manage to score a point or two by buying ice cream afterward. But back at home Willy once more banned her from his bath and climbed into Jace's lap for his bedtime story.

There was one thing different tonight, though. Once Willy was tucked in and Jace had kissed him goodnight, Clair summoned enough courage to bend over and give Willy a kiss of her own.

And Willy didn't protest.

Granted, he was nearly asleep, but it felt like a small victory to Clair just the same.

Then she and Jace stepped out of the little boy's room, and she was once again faced with the logical and natural conclusion to the evening.

And the desire for it not to end.

As they headed down the stairs, she silently ordered herself to say she was leaving, to say good-night. But somehow the words wouldn't take shape.

You're not here to be with Jace Brimley, she reminded herself. *You're here for Willy. You're here to* take Willy away from Jace Brimley. Spending time alone with him is the worst idea in the world.

"I'd better get going," she finally forced herself to say as they reached the entryway.

"You know you don't have to rush off. My bedtime isn't for a few hours yet."

It didn't help that his voice was like warm whisky seeping into her pores, lulling her, luring her and completely demolishing her already tenuous willpower.

"I wouldn't want to keep you from anything," she managed to say, but without much conviction.

"You wouldn't be keeping me from anything. And we could talk awhile. Get to know each other a little."

It was something they didn't do much of when Willy was awake because they were both paying attention to him. But the idea was very appealing now that Jace had presented it. Especially when Clair looked up at him, at the faint shadow of beard that had appeared as the day wore on, giving him a rough, rugged look that was so sexy....

"I'd like it if we got to know each other a little," she heard herself say in a voice softer than was appropriate.

But she did have things she wanted to ask him, she rationalized as temptation gained the upper hand. Things that pertained to Willy. Plus, getting to know Jace, letting Jace get to know her, might aid her cause. The friendlier they were, the better. It might go a long way toward making him realize that she was worthy of taking over custody of her nephew. The budding attraction to Jace himself didn't have anything to do with it.

Or so she tried to convince herself.

"I am curious about some things," she added. "Things I don't want to bring up around Willy in case he might overhear and get upset."

"Why don't we go into the living room, get comfortable and talk there?" Jace suggested.

There was nothing but friendliness and courtesy in his tone and even *that* was sexy when it came out in that deep baritone. Not to mention that the reference to getting comfortable conjured up a whole slew of images that Clair didn't want to think about.

"Okay," she agreed, despite what was going on in her body and mind as she tried to ignore the ripples of something primitively sensual.

"Want a cup of coffee or a soda or a glass of wine?" he asked as he motioned for her to precede him into the other room.

"No, thanks. I'm fine," she assured him, thinking that the wine they'd shared the previous night might have been the ultimate cause of that brief kiss she was determined not to repeat.

Clair sat at one end of the couch, pressing against the arm with her hip. It was exactly the opposite of where she wanted to be—which was in the middle of the sofa sitting as close to Jace as she did when they were in his truck.

Jace, on the other hand, seemed much more at ease with the situation and sat at an angle on the sofa so he was nearly facing her, one long arm stretched across the back, one thick leg up on the cushion with only his booted foot dangling off the edge.

"So what are you curious about?" he asked when they were settled.

It flashed through her mind that at that moment what she was most curious about was him. Probably because she'd never known anyone quite like him. Anyone who could care so tenderly for a child while still being such an elementally sexy, charming he-man.

But that wasn't a subject for discussion, so she worked to recall what she'd been referring to when she'd told him she was curious about some things.

"I'd just like to know the whole story behind how Kristin came to give up Willy to the Millers. And how—and why—you ended up with him."

"Fair enough. I'm not so sure where to start, though."

"How about with the Millers themselves?"

"Okay. Billy met Kim on a cruise ship. He entered a contest some juice company was having about eight years ago and won the grand prize. Kim was on the same cruise with some friends. If that wasn't fate takin' a hand I don't know what is."

"And it was love at first sight?"

"Pretty much. After ten days aboard ship they were already talkin' marriage. Two months later they tied the knot, decided they wanted kids right away and started what turned out to be nearly six years of tryin'."

"One of them was infertile?"

"Nobody ever figured that out. Separately they both

seemed fine but together they just never clicked. So they finally gave up and admitted that the only way they were likely to have a family was to adopt.''

''Isn't that usually a long process in itself?''

''Kim had an inheritance that left them in a financial position that helped speed things up. They could afford a private adoption, and an adoption lawyer hooked them up with Kristin.''

Her sister's sudden inclusion in the story seemed so cold, so clinical. Nothing more than a means to the Millers' end. At least that was how it seemed to Clair, even though that wasn't how Jace had said it, and it made her flinch internally.

''How far along was she by then?'' she asked quietly.

''About midway. She'd just turned eighteen, she was homeless and she said she'd learned that she couldn't take care of herself, let alone her baby.''

Sudden, unexpected tears flooded Clair's eyes as that internal flinch turned into plain, outright pain. Her sister had been homeless. Pregnant. No doubt scared silly. And at least in some part it was Clair's fault....

Apparently Jace saw the tears because he said, ''Are you sure you want to hear this?''

She didn't want to hear it. But suffering through hearing it was no more than she thought she deserved.

''Yes,'' she said firmly. ''Go on.''

''When Billy and Kim heard about how Kristin was living they paid her way here. She was in Billings. Apparently she'd hitchhiked from Chicago, wanting to go to California to a friend, but she'd had a scare with one of her rides and was afraid to go on doing that. Anyway, Billy and Kim took her in for the last half of the pregnancy.''

''To be their live-in baby factory.''

The words had spilled out, and only after they had did Clair realize how condemning they sounded. ''I'm sorry. I didn't mean that to be so snippy.''

Jace acknowledged the apology with a nod but went on to defend his friends, anyway.

''Billy and Kim wanted the baby and, yeah, that's how they came to be acquainted with Kristin. Their bringing her here is how we all got to know her. But Billy and Kim didn't for one minute just look at her as their baby factory.''

Clair cringed when he repeated the insensitive phrase.

''Takin' Kristin into their home wasn't what they had to do,'' he continued. ''They could have just put a roof over her head someplace else and still adopted Willy when he was born. They wanted to get to know Kristin. They wanted to help her. They wanted her to be in a loving, caring environment. And they didn't turn their backs on her once Willy was born—which they could have done and would have, if they'd only thought of her as a baby factory.''

''It was a poor choice of words,'' Clair said, trying to make amends.

It didn't help. Apparently Jace wasn't going to stop until he'd said his piece. ''They helped her finish high school here in town and, since she'd talked about wantin' to go to college, they got her scholarships and grants to pay her way there, too, and made sure she had enough money to get a place to live and start her off on her own. They would even have been happy if she'd come back here for holidays and visits, but Kristin opted for no contact once she was on her feet again. Otherwise I think they would have basically adopted Kristin, too.''

Clair knew she should be grateful. But she just felt guilty. And jealous. And resentful that other people—strangers—had provided what she would have liked to give her sister in Kristin's greatest hour of need. She didn't think she could bear to hear any more about how wonderful the Millers had been.

So she changed the subject.

''Well, I guess that's how the Millers got Willy. Now tell me how you ended up with him.''

But Jace didn't let her off the hook that easily. Instead of going on in that new vein, he said, ''You don't have to feel guilty, Clair.''

He was watching her closely, and it was as if those blue eyes of his could see everything she was feeling, everything she was thinking. As if he *knew*. It was bad enough that he was great looking, did he have to be all knowing, too?

''Sometimes it's easier to take help from folks who aren't family,'' he continued, even without confirmation that he was right. ''Kristin didn't have to feel as if she'd shamed or embarrassed anybody around here. She was honest about the fact that she'd done things she wasn't proud of. But she wanted to do what was right for her baby, and giving it up was what she thought was best.

"Still, it should have been me giving her the comfort and support she needed. She should never have been out on the streets. Homeless. Scared. *Hitchhiking...*"

"It wasn't your fault. She made the choice to run away."

Nothing he could say could make her feel better or absolve her, but she appreciated that he tried and just pressed him to move on.

"So tell me how you ended up with Willy," she repeated, trying to sound more cheery. "You must have been *really* good friends with his father."

Jace went on studying her for another long moment but finally he allowed the subject change.

"Billy's mom died of a heart attack when he was sixteen. Two years later—to the day—his father couldn't stand the grief he'd never gotten over and shot himself. It was September of our senior year of high school. Billy didn't have any other family, and since he was my best friend and hung out at the ranch as much as I hung out at his house, my parents had him come live with us. I guess my mom figured what was one more pair of smelly feet in a house full of them. If Billy and I hadn't been like brothers before that, we were after. We went off to college together, roomed together for those four years, then came back to the ranch."

"Billy came back to live with your family even after college?"

"Sure. He was welcome. We all considered him one of us. But then he got the itch to be sheriff and bought this place." Jace glanced around the living room. "He married Kim about six months later. I was best man at their wedding and got to be friends with Kim, too. 'Course I got married about the same time, so the four of us—"

"You were married?"

"Until about a year ago," he answered, but there was an unusual curtness to his voice that warned her he didn't want to talk about it. "Anyway, I was as close a friend as I could be to the two of them, and after they got Willy they decided they'd better make out a will and choose a guardian for him in case anything ever happened to both of them. By then Kristin was long gone and no one knew where she was. But they felt confident she would make something of herself, so they thought she should have the chance to have Willy back if she wanted him. And if she didn't, then I was to be his guardian. I guess it was just more of fate takin' a hand that she died just when she could have had that chance."

"And you got to be a daddy by default," Clair said, repeating Rennie's words of that morning.

It made Jace laugh. "That about sums it up. Mostly I look at it as a sort of blessing to help make up for losin' Billy."

Clair definitely didn't want to think in terms of *that*. Not when taking Willy away was on her agenda.

"Does Willy seem to miss his mom and dad?" she asked then.

"It was worse at first," he said. "And confusing. Kim was killed instantly but Billy was in a coma for four months, so first I had to try to explain that his mom wasn't coming back and that his dad was really, really sick. But it was all basically over his head. He'd still ask where his mom and dad were, call for them. One night he kept wandering from room to room looking for them—that broke my heart. And then Billy died and I had to say his dad had gone to heaven with his mom—still not a concept he understood. But most of it has stopped now. He'll still ask about them sometimes, as if he's testing me to see if he gets the same answer, but for the most part he's adapted. He's feeling more and more secure. More and more comfortable with the way things have ended up. He's pretty settled with me."

Clair had the sense that there was an underlying message for her in Jace's words. A message that she could be doing Willy a disservice by rocking the boat for him again.

But she held fast to the thought that the more comfortable Willy got with her, the less that would be the case. Because knowing just what her sister had gone through after leaving Clair's apartment that last time only solidified her determination to make amends by raising her sister's child.

But it was too soon yet to get into that with Jace. So when the grandfather clock in the corner of the room chimed the hour, she used that as her cue.

"I didn't realize it was so late. I should go," she said, standing.

Jace stood, too, and as he did Clair said, "Thanks for filling me in."

"None of it was a secret," he assured her on the way to the front door.

"No, but you didn't have to bother."

"Talkin' to you isn't a bother, Clair. I like it. I like you."

That last part surprised her, and when she looked up at Jace as they stopped in the entryway, she had the impression that saying it had surprised him almost as much.

Or maybe the surprise was in the realization that he meant it.

Clair didn't know how to respond, though. It seemed odd to say she liked him in return, despite the fact that she did. Much more than she wished she did.

But instead she seized upon something else she was getting to know more and more about him with each passing day. "You're a good man, Jace."

"Ooo," he said, joking and scrunching up his handsome face as if he'd just taken a punch. "Is that another way of saying I'm a nice guy? Because everybody knows *that's* the kiss of death."

Clair laughed. "No, it isn't another way of saying you're a nice guy, but you're that, too. And I don't think it's the kiss of death." But kissing was most certainly on her mind again as they stood there at the site of the kiss he'd given her the previous night.

"Don't kid a kidder," he went on teasing. "I know you women all like bad boys."

"And from the look in your eyes I can tell there's

some of that in you, too,'' she said, flirting without meaning to.

''I'm a good man *and* a bad boy?''

''Actually,'' she said with a laugh as she thought about that, ''I think that's exactly what you are. The man in you is good, but the boy? Watch out for him.''

Jace seemed to like that, because he smiled a slow, pleased and very sexy smile.

''Then watch out,'' he warned in a husky voice just before he leaned over and kissed her.

It took her so off guard that she almost pulled away out of reflex.

But she caught herself before she did and stayed for the kiss.

Stayed? She did more than merely stay. After that initial, instantaneous shock, she kissed him back.

And tonight she really had the chance to kiss him back because, unlike the night before, this wasn't only a brief peck. This was a kiss. A full-on, lingering kiss that let her actually feel the hot, supple smoothness of his lips. That let her feel the slight scratch of his beard. That let her breathe in deeply of the clean woodsy scent of his aftershave.

And, oh, how she liked it all!

She let her head fall back enough for him to kiss her even more deeply. She let her lips part in answer to the gentle persuasion of his. And she most definitely kissed him back!

But even though this was a real kiss, it still ended before she wanted it to. Before she was ready for it to.

Of course, she wasn't sure she would *ever* have been ready for it to end.

But she felt him drawing it to a close. Slowly. Reluctantly? But to a close nonetheless.

"I have to stop doing that," he said when his mouth finally abandoned hers. But the low, raspy tone of his voice and the glint of pure deviltry in his eyes, in his smile, made her doubt that he meant it.

"Yeah," she agreed, although with a dreamy-sounding sigh.

"Tomorrow we're at the ranch again," Jace said then, changing the subject but still using the intimate tone that seemed to wrap around her and hold her mesmerized. "Are you interested?"

Silly question. There didn't seem to be anything about him she *wasn't* interested in....

"Just tell me when."

"After lunch? I have some things I need to take care of around here first."

"Perfect."

Perfect? Had she actually said that? And, again, in that dreamy voice? As if tagging along with him and Willy to do ranch work was the best way she could possibly think to spend a day? Maybe she was losing her marbles.

"Come over a little after noon, then," he instructed.

He hadn't touched her with anything but his lips, and even as they stood in the entryway, his hands were in his back pockets. Yet Clair still felt held there just by his gaze.

"Okay," she agreed, and then she put some effort

into tearing her eyes away from his. Into moving to the door and opening it.

"Thanks," she said. Then she wondered if it sounded as if she were thanking him for the kiss and added, "For today and tonight and everything."

"Nothin' to thank me for."

Again his voice was deep, husky, intimate, and the intensity, the potency, of his charm mixed with the pure gorgeousness of him was enough to knock her socks off. Enough to make her want to throw herself into his arms and have him kiss her again and again. Have him do a whole lot more than kiss her. Enough to make her forget herself and why she was there and everything else in her life.

But she couldn't do that and she knew it. So she made herself step through the door and say goodnight.

"'Night," Jace answered.

Clair waved a hand over her shoulder but didn't give him so much as a backward glance because she knew that was all it would take to make her forget everything again and give in to what she was beginning to want as much as she wanted to make amends for failing her sister, as much as she wanted to raise her nephew.

Just one more glance was all it would take to make her forget everything again and give in to wanting Jace....

Chapter Five

"Harry. Thanks for getting back to me so quick," Jace said into the phone at eleven the next morning after the lawyer's secretary announced that it was Mr. Aronson calling. Harry Aronson was the estate attorney who had made out Billy's and Kim's wills.

"No problem," the lawyer said in a high-pitched voice that belied his 280-pound weight and the expertise that earned him $175 an hour. "How is everything?"

"On the surface? Great. But I'm not sure what might be brewing *under* the surface," Jace said, thinking that wasn't altogether true. Part of what was brewing under the surface—at least under his surface—he recognized. Attraction—*intense* attraction—to Clair. Intense attraction to Clair that he wished he were fighting more successfully than he was.

But what was under *her* surface was the point of the phone call to the attorney.

"Willy's birth mother's sister has shown up," Jace said.

"Uh-huh," Harry responded noncommittally.

"She's a nice woman. Great, in fact. I like her." A lot. Too much. "And she hasn't come right out and said she wants custody of Willy. But I'm getting the feeling that's why she's here." Among so many other feelings he was getting in response to Clair. Feelings that were all the more treacherous and unwise if he was right about why she was in Elk Creek.

"Is she married?" the attorney asked.

"No."

"Engaged to be married? Divorced?"

"I don't know." And it surprised him to realize the truth in that, since the feelings he had for her made it seem as if he knew her better than he actually did.

But knowing she had the sweetest lips in four states and smelled better than fresh-baked apple pie wasn't going to do him much good.

"I don't think she's engaged." Or she probably wouldn't be letting him kiss her and kissing him back with so much enthusiasm. "Does it matter?"

"Everything matters if it comes to a custody battle."

"I think she's more a career woman than anything, if that helps." Not that a woman being intensely focussed on her career had done anything but hurt Jace in the past.

"The court could just say that means she can provide for the child financially."

Great. So it *could* hurt him again.

"Wasn't there a rift in that family?" Harry asked. "If I'm remembering right, without the file in front of me, wasn't the birth mother out on the streets? Didn't the Millers take her in?"

"You're remembering right," Jace confirmed, but it gnawed at him to do it. He'd seen the pain in Clair over that rift with her sister, and it didn't seem right to use it against her. Even if he had to. "I think that's what's motivating this. Clair has a lot of guilt over a falling-out with Kristin. I figure that she wants to make up for what she sees as having failed her and that she wants to do it through Willy."

"Hard to predict how that will go over with a judge. We could use it as the reason she *shouldn't* be granted custody—say that if she was so concerned and caring she would have helped her sister when her sister needed it. But her side could say guilt is why she'd go to extra lengths to be a good parent, and a judge might agree. I'll tell you one thing—and you should know that child custody is not my specialty so I'd have to pass you off to the partner who handles that—but I think if this aunt is willing to sue for custody we could have a real fight ahead of us. Yes, it helps that you were the parents' choice to raise their son if the birth mother was out of the picture, and I would testify to their strong feelings on the matter, but an unrelated single man as opposed to a female blood relative is not the most ideal case. It's anybody's guess which way a court might rule.''

"That's what I was afraid of.''

"Where's she from?''

"Chicago.''

"So she's come a long way to see the boy.''

"Yeah.''

"Has she made any noises about taking him home with her? Like even for a visit?''

"No. And Willy won't give her the time of day. She's just workin' at gettin' him to warm up to her.''

"Well don't encourage it. In fact, you're better off keeping as much distance from the woman as possible. Beyond that, all I can tell you is to wait and see, and if she makes a move for custody we'll go to war.''

Jace thanked the attorney for the consultation and hung up. But it left him with a sour taste in his mouth.

He knew the lawyer was only looking out for his and Willy's best interests, but the idea of not allowing Clair free access to Willy, discouraging a relationship between the two of them, didn't sit well with him.

Maybe from a legal standpoint it was the best thing to do, but from a moral standpoint he wasn't sure it was the *right* thing to do. Clair *was* Willy's aunt, after all. Should he be deprived of a connection he might eventually appreciate or even long for? A connection with a blood relative?

And what about Clair? Willy was the only nephew she would ever have. Shouldn't she be allowed to know him? To have a part in his life as she had said she wanted to when she'd first arrived in Elk Creek?

Jace thought she should. He thought both Willy and Clair should have the benefits of their blood tie.

And if the worst possible scenario actually came to be, if he lost Willy to Clair, wouldn't it be better for Willy to know her? To like her? To be comfortable with her? Rather than to be handed over to someone Jace had kept a stranger?

He just hoped it didn't come to that, Jace thought as he returned to replacing the washer on the faucet at the kitchen sink.

Still, the attorney's words about keeping her at a distance rang through his head.

But he wasn't even sure that getting custody of Willy was what Clair wanted, he reminded himself. She hadn't come out and said that was why she was here. It was possible that being a part of Willy's life and Willy being a part of hers, that wanting to make up for what happened between her and Kristin, could just mean that she wanted to be a good, long-distance aunt to the boy. And nothing more.

Except that the longer she was in Elk Creek, the longer Jace spent with her and saw how desperate she was to connect with Willy, the more he felt sure she had an ulterior motive.

And that that ulterior motive was to take Willy away and raise him herself.

So why the hell didn't he do what the lawyer had advised and get some distance from her?

He had to admit that it wasn't only because he thought it was wrong not to allow the contact between Willy and Clair. There was also his own attraction to her. Those two kisses couldn't be denied, and they certainly hadn't come out of any kind of moral righteousness. They'd come out of the weak spot he had for Clair herself.

The same weak spot he'd had for Stephanie.

A weak spot for the women he should avoid. Women who had goals diametrically opposed to his own.

He thought he'd learned his lesson, but apparently getting burned once wasn't enough. Because here he was again, hip-deep in who-knew-what with a woman he shouldn't even be friendly with.

And just what was he hip-deep in with Clair? he asked himself.

A couple of innocent kisses weren't too serious all by themselves, but he knew he was kidding himself if he believed that was all there was to it.

He was feeling things he didn't want to be feeling. Stirrings that were hardly innocent. Especially when kissing her wasn't all he wanted to do with her, and both of the last two nights he'd taken to bed with him some hot and wild fantasies of what else he wanted to do with her....

But that, at least, he should stop.

It might be wrong for him not to let her have access to Willy, but he didn't have to get into anything personal with her.

And he *shouldn't* be getting into anything personal with her.

Because then he was giving her double the ammunition. Double the opportunity to hurt him by not only taking Willy away from him, but by leaving him behind the way Stephanie had. And he didn't think he could go through that again.

Which meant that even if he wasn't going to put any physical distance between Willy and Clair, he should still put some emotional distance between himself and Clair.

Some emotional distance that ruled out kissing, for starters.

But even though that all seemed logical and wise and was surely the best course of action, Jace was still leery.

Because he knew himself. He knew what Clair was churning up in him. He knew just how attracted he was to her and how powerless he was to control that attraction when he was with her. And he was worried that he wouldn't be able to resist her.

So maybe the truth of it was that he'd already rolled the dice by letting her into both his and Willy's lives this far and it was too late to turn back now.

He'd just have to wait and see how those dice came up.

But it didn't sit well with him.

It didn't sit well with him at all....

"There's a storm brewin'. Weatherman is predictin' a spring blizzard, and those can do as much as or more damage than winter ones. So we're droppin' bales of hay for the horses and cattle out on the range in case we can't get back to 'em for a while," Jace explained as he loaded the square bales onto his truck bed early that afternoon.

Willy was making a serious show of helping by picking up handfuls of fallen hay and throwing them onto the truck in much the same way. Except that most of Willy's handfuls ended up on the ground rather than in the truck bed.

Clair was enjoying both shows—the little boy imitating the man and the man. Oh, the man! Thigh muscles straining his jeans as he used his legs to bear the weight of the hay. Narrow waist twisting from hay pile to truck and back again. Biceps bulging through chambray shirt and jean jacket as he grabbed each bale, hoisted it and tossed it as if it weighed next to nothing.

The sky was blue-gray with low-hanging ominous-looking clouds that somehow seemed to bring out the color. The wind that was whipping around kept blowing his collar up over the close-cut line of golden-oak hair at his nape.

All in all, the world seemed about to erupt into violence, and he looked capable of taming it if it did.

"Can I help?" Clair asked, thinking that doing something besides huddling inside her own wool winter coat, tunic sweater and jeans might distract her from his appeal.

The offer caused a slow grin on Jace's heart-poundingly handsome face. "Think you can lift one of these?" he challenged as if the very thought amused him.

"I don't know," she answered honestly, moving to the stack inside the lean-to.

It was well down so she didn't have to reach above hip-level for a bale. But when she did, she misjudged just how heavy it was and barely managed to raise it an inch off the one beneath it before losing her grip and letting it fall back in place.

That made Jace chuckle. "Heavier than that ad copy I imagine you're usually hauling around, aren't they?"

"Is there something else I could do?" she asked, also not thrilled with what the hay did to her ungloved hands.

"How about putting Willy in his car seat to get him out of this wind before it chaps his face? I'll be done here in a minute and we can go."

"Okay."

Jace's attention switched to the little boy, who was making more of a mess than helping. "That's enough now, Willy. Climb into your seat and let Clair buckle you up."

"Wanna hep you," Willy protested.

"You've helped me enough. Now go do what I said."

Willy had actually returned Clair's "Hi," when she'd arrived after lunch, and now she was pleased to see that he didn't balk too much at the order to let her buckle his seat belt.

"What a big boy you are," she cooed as he climbed into the truck, onto the seat and finally landed in his car seat. "And you're a good helper, too," she added, shamelessly praising him in hopes of winning him over with flattery.

"Yep," he answered as if she were stating the obvious and he didn't have much regard for her intelligence. But the fact that he was talking to her at all seemed like progress.

Of course it didn't help her intellectual standing when she couldn't figure out which strap went where or buckled into what and the tiny child had to point and say, "It goes dare." But at least he wasn't screaming for her to get away from him.

"Do you like the horses and cows, Willy?" she tried again, staying in the lee of the passenger door with one foot on the runner.

"Yep."

"Ask him what sound the cows make," Jace advised from the back of the truck where his rhythm went uninterrupted.

"What sound do the cows make?" she repeated.

"Moo-oo," Willy complied with gusto.

Clair laughed, hoping it wouldn't offend him. "That's very good. How about the horses? Do you know what sound they make?"

The toddler whinnied comically, and Clair laughed again. "You're great!"

"Do the monkey now, Willy," Jace coached from the rear.

Willy not only whoo-whooed, he also scratched under his arm this time, and once more Clair rewarded him with a laugh—something Willy seemed pleased to inspire in her.

"How 'bout the cat and the dog?" this from Jace again.

"Meow. Woof-woof."

"And the bird?"

"Chup, chup."

"The snake?"

"Husss."

Clair laughed and applauded, exulting as much in her nephew's performance as in the fact that he seemed to be proud of his ability to entertain her.

"Now Unca Ace," the little boy said then, loud enough for Jace to hear.

Jace laughed. "I think you covered everything," he said.

"Now Unca Ace," Willy insisted, giving each word a slow pronunciation, as if Jace might not have understood before.

"You make sounds, too?" Clair called back to him.

"Where do you think Willy learned them?" he bragged.

"Do yion," Willy commanded.

"You do the lion," Jace countered.

Willy roared on cue, then said, "Do hairy monser."

But apparently Jace had anticipated that one because all of a sudden he wasn't at the truck bed anymore. He'd come around the other side of the vehicle to spring up from behind, making horrible growling-roaring-raging noises and pouncing on both Willy and Clair at once.

Clair hadn't seen him coming and jumped in fright while Willy giggled riotously.

"Sca-wed you," he accused.

"Scared," Jace translated in her ear, his breath

warm and much too arousing there, as he, too, laughed at her.

But Clair didn't mind being the butt of the joke. She was too glad to be included and to have Willy just acknowledging her existence.

"Come on, scaredy-cat, let's get you in the truck so we can go," Jace said then, checking the seat belts on Willy's seat before ushering Clair around to the driver's side.

For some reason, this time he helped her into the truck's cab with his hands at her waist. He'd never done it before—in fact it was the first time he'd touched her at all, despite having kissed her twice now. But it was as if the levity the three of them had just shared had opened a door on camaraderie, on an almost family-type closeness that made it seem natural to have that physical contact.

But natural or not, the trouble was that his big, strong hands felt so good she didn't want him to take them away. And when he did a tiny bubble of elation deflated inside her.

Still, though, that revelry and that touch set the tone for the drive they embarked on. Jace continued instigating games that Willy was familiar with, games that taught him things like colors and counting and the alphabet. He also didn't hesitate to nudge Clair with his shoulder or make other contact that, although inconsequential, was physical contact nonetheless and kept pumping air back into that bubble, keeping her spirits and her enjoyment level high.

As they traveled to the farthest reaches of the Brimley property Clair began to realize that not only didn't the Brimleys' farmhouse compare favorably with the larger and more elaborate homes of their neighbors, but that their holdings weren't all that impressive, either. From the fences they encountered along the way, it seemed to Clair that their neighbors owned parcels that narrowed the Brimley property considerably, finally cutting it off completely.

"Am I wrong or do those fences mean your neighbors are trying to swallow you up?" she asked when Jace had unloaded the last of the bales of hay and returned to the truck cab where Willy had fallen asleep in his car seat.

"They've come pretty close," he confirmed.

Clair recalled Jace mentioning that the Brimley ranch wasn't up to par with the others in the area, but at the time he'd seemed not to want to talk about it. Now she wondered if the reason he didn't want to talk about it was that his neighbors were edging him out.

She wasn't sure if she should pursue the subject since he'd already avoided it once.

Then, as if he were reading her thoughts, he said, "It isn't the way you made it sound, though. They aren't the bigger fish layin' in wait for a weak moment so they can devour us. The Culhanes and the Hellers years ago, and the McDermots more recently, have actually bought up land to help us out—much to my father's regret when he was alive. But the man—good as he was as a father—never could make a go of things around here himself."

"Why not?" Clair ventured.

"He grew up here and inherited the place from my grandparents. They bought the land and built a small house when they got married, and even though it wasn't a huge spread, they made a living. But when my father took over he wasn't satisfied with that. He wanted everything on a grander scale. A big family. A big house. He was always tryin' to be a *contender,* as he called it. But he risked too much along the way rather than tendin' to business the way he should have.''

"A contender with your neighbors?"

"Yep. Back before the last few years the McDermot place was owned by their grandfather—Buzz Martindale. When Buzz was workin' it, it was on a par with us, so my father wasn't competing with him. The Culhanes and the Hellers were the thorn in his side. Call it poor management or just bad luck, but my dad couldn't keep up with them. Year after year they'd bring in better grain prices or more per head of cattle or make a big sale on a brood mare while my dad was barely makin' ends meet. So he started lookin' for somethin' that would make him get rich quick."

"Never a good thing."

"Definitely not the way my dad went about it. He would overplant and produce even more inferior product, or plant some hare-brained crops that wouldn't sell at all. Or he'd put too many animals on too little ground and without enough feed they'd be too scrawny to even take to market. He even tried turnin' the place into a dude ranch, of all things. Boy, was *that* a bust. And every time he failed, he'd have to sell off more of the land my grandfather had started with to bail us out and put food on the table."

"Did he resent having to turn to his neighbors?" Clair said, guessing that might have had something to do with Jace's earlier reluctance to discuss this.

"He resented them mightily for everything. For their success. For having to go to them for help. For having to work as a ranch hand for them when times were really tough. Like I said, he was a great father, but the man himself? When you said your father has a chip on his shoulder, you could have been talkin' about mine. A big enough chip on his shoulder that I think it put him right into an early grave frettin' and fussin' over everything."

"How are things going now?"

"Better. My brothers and I are slowly rebuilding our holdings by keeping our noses to the grindstone and sticking to the tried-and-true."

"It must not be easy, though," she said, "trying to recover from years of failures."

"No, it isn't easy. By the time my father died we were on the brink of losin' everything. But we've brought the ranch back from that point, and now we're lookin' toward the day when we can expand. We do all the work among the five of us rather than hirin' any help and that lets us save."

"And the neighbors? Are they willing to sell when you get the money together?"

"For the most part. There are a few acres that didn't go to the Hellers or the McDermots or the Culhanes, and the folks who own those aren't too willing to give 'em up. But those three have told us that they looked at their purchases as collateral for loans to the family and they'll let us have back whatever we can afford along the way.''

''That's really nice of them.''

''My father wouldn't have seen it like that. He'd have said they were lookin' down their noses at us, that they were treatin' us like charity cases, takin' pity on us. He probably wouldn't have accepted the land back at all.''

''How do you and your brothers feel about it?''

That creased his brow and darkened his expression to such a degree that Clair was afraid she'd ventured too far.

But after a moment he admitted, ''It's tough on the pride. We all grew up and went to school with the Culhanes and the Hellers. Some of us found better friends among them than others of us did. But it isn't easy when one minute you're in class with them, horsin' around on an even field, and then school gets out and they're hittin' the Dairy King to flirt with the girls while you're goin' to work for their father alongside yours.''

''That would be hard for teenage kids,'' Clair commiserated.

''Plus there's the small-town element. Everybody knows everybody else's business. So even if it didn't come from the Hellers or the Culhanes or a lot of folks around here, there was still that contingent that would talk and ridicule. More than once I've overheard some nasty remark about my father's latest 'fool-headed scheme.' That's not easy to handle anytime, but definitely not when you're a kid. My brother Devon—''

"He's the one who's a veterinarian?" Clair interrupted to make sure she was remembering right.

"Yeah, the vet," Jace confirmed. "Devon always thought we should sell out completely and start over somewhere else."

"Is that why he isn't here now?"

"Partially. There's more to it than that—Devon and Scott had a pretty bad falling out over a woman, and that's why he left for good about a year ago. But, yeah, feeling like Elk Creek's poor relatives didn't help."

"And what about you? Did you have to swallow your pride a lot or did you find friends among the Hellers and the Culhanes?"

"Both. I consider Jackson Heller and Clint Culhane good friends, but I've swallowed my fair share of pride, too," he said. Then, after a moment he added gravely, "I'll tell you one thing, though, I'll like it when my mother quits workin' as a housekeeper."

"She's unhappy working for the McDermots?" It seemed odd to refer to people she hadn't even met as if she knew them, but she wanted Jace to know she'd listened to the things he'd said along the way and remembered them—one of them being that his mother worked for the McDermot family.

"No, she's not unhappy working for them," Jace answered. "Far from it. They treat her like one of the family, and she feels comfortable enough with them to give 'em what-for just the same as she does me and my brothers. But she's not young anymore, and it's tiring to take care of two households. I want to see her only taking care of her own. But we can't even mention her quittin' without gettin' our heads bit off. She won't believe we don't need the money she brings in anymore.''

"Maybe she likes feeling useful and having the independence that earning her own money gives her," Clair suggested.

"That's what she says."

"But you don't believe it?"

They were nearly in town again, since they'd gone directly from the last hay drop to the main road back to Elk Creek. As Jace slowed to the lower speed limit he said, "I think she just says it so we won't feel bad about her workin' and so we don't have to pick up any more of the slack moneywise."

"Or she could mean it. Working could make her feel productive and needed. Or are you a Neanderthal who doesn't think a woman should work outside the home?"

That made him smile. "A Neanderthal?"

Clair raised a challenging eyebrow at him but merely waited for him to answer her question.

"No, I'm not a Neanderthal who thinks women shouldn't work outside their home. I do think, though, that when a woman gets to the point of needin' to soak her feet and sit with a heating pad on her back every night she's doin' too much."

"But before that it's okay if she works?"

"Sure. But I also think that if it can be done, financially, it's good for mothers to stay home with their kids. If that makes me a Neanderthal, then pass the club and point me to the woolly mammoth.''

Jace in a loincloth?

Clair fought the instant mental image and the increase in her pulse rate that went with it.

''What if the mother has a career she loves and she *wants* to work?''

''Then, if it's financially possible, I think the dad should stay home with the kids.''

''So we're back to that anti-institutional thing again.''

Jace merely smiled at her as he pulled into the driveway and came to a stop. ''Guess so,'' he said as if he'd enjoyed the debate but hadn't changed any of his views because of it.

''You're hopeless,'' she said on a frustrated sigh.

That stretched his smile into a grin and made Clair wonder how much of his taking the line of opposition was just to get her goat.

He turned off the engine and, rather than open the door the way Clair expected him to, he pivoted in her direction, reached one arm along the back of the seat and the other across the dashboard, effectively enclosing her in the U of his big body. ''Want to argue politics and religion now?'' he asked with that devilish glint in his denim-blue eyes.

''Why? There's no changing your mind about anything.''

He leaned forward enough to brush her ear again with his breath. ''But it's so much fun tryin'.''

''Says who?''

"I'm enjoyin' myself."

Okay, so she was enjoying herself, too. But she wasn't going to concede that point, either.

Instead she nodded in the direction of the house next door. "I should get over there and help Rennie with dinner."

Jace didn't budge. He just went on watching her, smiling a Cheshire Cat smile now. "I almost forgot we were all havin' dinner there tonight."

"So Willy can play with Rennie's niece while Rennie is baby-sitting her."

"And here I was wastin' time tryin' to think of what you and I could do tonight."

He made that sound very lascivious, and Clair wasn't sure if he was teasing her or not. "Well now you don't have to. We're spending the evening with Rennie and her niece."

She hadn't intended for that to sound so couple-ish but that's the way it had come out.

Jace didn't seem to mind. He didn't even comment on it. "And afterward maybe you can read the bedtime story tonight," he added, but again with a note in his voice that hinted at something more intimate.

Clair tried to ignore the tingle of delight his tone created in her. She tried just to concentrate on the fact that she was being automatically included in the bedtime ritual and wouldn't have to come up with a way to get herself invited from Rennie's house back to Jace's at the end of the evening as she'd thought she might.

"I'd like that," she told him, referring to his offer

to let her read the story. "But I really should get over there and help now," she added since he still hadn't moved and, in fact, seemed to be keeping her captive between the wall of his muscular male body and Willy asleep in the car seat.

Clair wasn't exactly sure why, though, and what flashed through her mind was that maybe he was going to kiss her again.

But would he do that right out in the open? In broad—if waning—daylight? On the driveway where anyone could see them?

She doubted it. But she was also surprised to find that she wouldn't mind if he did. That she wouldn't mind where he kissed her just so long as he kissed her....

But instead, after a slight chuckle, Jace turned around, opened the door and got out of the truck, dashing her hopes just that quickly.

"Okay, fine, desert us," he joked, holding out a hand to her as if she might need help getting out behind him.

And even though they both knew she didn't, Clair slipped her hand into his, anyway, just so she could finally feel his skin against hers.

Warm, leathery-soft, strong—just the way she'd imagined it would be when she was lying in her bed the last few nights, thinking about how his hand might feel on the rest of her body.

He kept hold of her even after she was out of the truck. And, in fact, he caught and held her eyes, too, delving into them, setting off sparks that seemed out of proportion to such a simple thing.

Then he let go of her. Of her hand. Of her gaze. Releasing her like a tractor beam turned off.

"Guess I'll see you at Rennie's in an hour or so," he said, and the only indication that they might have shared a moment of quiet intimacy was in the deeper, huskier timbre of his voice.

"Yeah, I think she's planning to eat around six," Clair responded mindlessly, trying to regain her bearings.

But even as she forced her feet to move to take her across the yards to the house next door, Clair marveled at the pure power the man could so easily wield over her and her own lack of ability to resist it. To resist him.

She'd never had that problem before. Not even with Lyle. Not with any man.

But then, something was different about Jace all the way around. Different about the things he brought to life in her.

The plain and honest truth of the matter was that it would have been so much easier to resist his power over her, to resist the man himself, if only she didn't like him so much....

Chapter Six

"Do you baby-sit every Friday night?" Clair asked as she and Rennie were putting the finishing touches on dinner and waiting for Jace and Willy to arrive.

"I wouldn't if I had a hot date or something. But that hasn't happened since I've moved to Elk Creek so, yes, I've been baby-sitting every Friday night. I don't mind, though. I enjoy our sleep-overs as much as Lissa does, so it gives me something to look forward to all week. And then my brother and his wife get a date night, which is good for them, too."

Rennie was filling glasses with ice and water, and when she was finished and putting them on a tray, she said, "Speaking of Lissa, I'd better check on her and see if she's still keeping busy with her new play kitchen—my brother will shoot me when he finds out

I bought her such an elaborate present for no reason at all. He thinks I spoil her. But what else are aunts for?''

They're for raising their nieces or nephews if the parents can't, Clair thought.

But as Rennie picked up the tray of water glasses and left the room, Clair's mind wandered beyond her hostess's parting comment and her own secret motive for being in Elk Creek to Rennie's earlier reference to a date night.

A date night—what an appealing idea.

A date night with Jace....

She was crazy about Willy. Even if he wasn't so crazy about her and had only advanced to the point of tolerating her. She loved watching him when he was busy and absorbed with something. She loved seeing how his mind worked. She loved the way he talked and the funny things he said and did. Her commitment to winning him over and taking him with her back to Chicago was only strengthening with every minute she spent with him and saw more and more of Kristin in him.

But the thought of leaving him with a sitter for just a few hours and going out alone with Jace, maybe for a candlelit dinner and dancing afterward? Oh, what she wouldn't give for that guilty pleasure!

And she did feel guilty about it. The last thing she should be thinking about was a man. She'd just come out of a relationship that hadn't been good for her, a relationship in which she'd had to make all the compromises. She certainly didn't need the complications of another relationship—one that would be even more complicated than the last. Especially not when her real focus was on Willy.

Which meant that she shouldn't be pining for Jace or fantasizing about a date with him.

But it seemed as if the harder she tried not to pine for him, the more she pined for him, anyway. And the fantasies? Fantasizing about a date was by far the least of her fantasies about Jace!

She knew the best thing that could happen was that Willy would suddenly fall in love with her and she could use his attachment to her as the reason why she should be the one to raise him. Then she could be up-front with Jace and get back to Chicago. Out of harm's way.

But since that didn't seem about to happen, she really needed to exercise some restraint, she told herself.

For instance, she had to stop thinking about him kissing her, longing for him to kiss her, every time he barely looked at her—as he had today in the truck when they'd returned from the ranch.

But when a faint sound from the living room made her perk up and listen intently to hear if Jace and Willy were arriving, and as her pulse raced and every ounce of her went on the alert at the possibility, she knew that she was at odds with herself. Because no matter what she thought intellectually, no matter what lessons she'd just learned from Lyle, emotionally she was so vulnerable to Jace that a part of her seemed to have a whole different agenda, an agenda that made her feel like a helpless victim to her attraction to him.

And nothing she did or thought or decided or vowed seemed to help.

"Lissa's fine," Rennie said, interrupting Clair's musings as she came back into the small, pale-blue kitchen.

Apparently the sound Clair had thought she heard wasn't Jace and Willy arriving, which left her with two reactions—relief that she didn't have to deal with the unwanted attraction to Jace yet, and disappointment that he wasn't there.

She really was at odds with herself.

Then Rennie seemed to take a second look at Clair and said, "I just noticed how nice you look. You're all dressed up."

"Well, this is a dinner party," Clair demurred, hoping that seemed like enough of an excuse.

"A dinner party for two-year-olds," Rennie qualified with a laugh.

Clair just hoped her hostess didn't guess that it hadn't been the two year olds she'd been thinking about when she'd taken a second shower after leaving Jace in the driveway. When she'd washed her hair and reapplied her makeup. Or that it had been with Jace in mind that she'd pulled her hair back in tiny, glittery clips she'd positioned around her head like a headband and opted to wear her tightest black, stretchy capri pants and split V-necked yellow lycra T-shirt and the strappy three-inch heels that went with them.

The doorbell rang just then and, when Rennie left the kitchen again to answer it, Clair followed behind with the now-full bread basket. This time she wasn't just hearing things, she knew Jace and Willy were there, so she hurried to set the basket on the dining room table and went the rest of the way into the living room to be there when Rennie let them in.

"Wow! Looks like I'm underdressed tonight," Rennie said almost the moment she opened the door.

Clair came up beside her as Jace and Willy stepped across the threshold, and it was apparent that she wasn't the only one who had seized the opportunity to spruce up for tonight.

Jace had changed into a pair of black jeans and a matching black Western shirt with a bright splash of red, yellow and orange Aztec design in a stripe across his broad chest. Even Willy was in dressier-than-usual corduroy jeans and a knit shirt that buttoned up the front.

Rennie was right, in her everyday jeans and simple crew-neck sweater, she did seem underdressed. Or maybe the rest of them were *over*dressed.

"Hi, guys," Clair greeted. She wasn't sure where the possessiveness in her tone had come from, but there it was, anyway.

Jace returned her hello, his blue eyes giving her a quick once-over before an appreciative, secret sort of smile lifted one corner of his mouth.

He was freshly shaven, too. And he smelled of just enough aftershave to make Clair's head go light when she caught a whiff of it.

"Lissa? Come say hi to our guests," Rennie called to where her little towheaded niece was busy with a plastic rendition of a kitchen, complete with pots, pans and play food to cook, serve and clean up after.

Only when Rennie drew her attention specifically did the toddler glance up. But when she did, her big brown eyes lit up with joy and she made a beeline for the rest of the group.

"Jace!" she nearly shrieked like an obsessed fan who had spotted a rock star.

"Hi, Miss Lissa," Jace responded warmly while Rennie whispered to Clair, "Lissa has a little crush on Jace."

A *little* crush? Clair thought the crush was bigger than the child as Lissa clamped her arms around his leg and pressed her cheek to the outside of his thigh in utter bliss.

So, okay, maybe flinging her arms around Jace with uninhibited abandon was something Clair might have liked to do herself if she'd had the chance. But witnessing Lissa's response to him still made her feel awkward.

Apparently, it did the same thing to Rennie because she laughed with some embarrassment and tried to urge her niece away. "Come on, Lissa, let go of Jace. He can't walk with you hanging on to his leg."

"It's okay. Everybody should have such a warm welcome," Jace said graciously, taking it in his stride.

He bent over to pick up the tiny girl and held her on his hip the way he usually held Willy. "It's good to see you, too, Lissa," he said, making light of the child's show of affection.

Lissa said something Clair didn't understand at all

but Jace seemed to because when the child pointed to her new play set he said, "Excuse me, ladies, I'm being given the grand tour." Then he took Lissa and Willy to the toy kitchen.

"We'll get dinner on the table," Rennie suggested.

Jace was still the guest of honor at Lissa's private party when the spaghetti, meatballs and salad were on the table, and he had to coax both kids to come eat since Willy was as enamored of the play set as Lissa was.

Not surprisingly, Lissa insisted on sitting next to Jace and having him help her with her food.

"I really didn't invite you over here tonight to baby-sit for me," Rennie apologized.

But again Jace didn't seem to mind. The man was just a Pied Piper with kids, Clair decided, feeling slightly better about Willy's rejection of her in favor of Jace since Lissa was doing the same thing to her aunt.

Still, though, as the evening wore on, Jace's attention was almost completely usurped by Lissa and Willy, and Clair began to find herself missing his company and longing for the dinner party to come to an end so she could get next door with just Jace and Willy again.

Luckily both two-year-olds had early bedtimes, and by eight o'clock Jace announced that the pretend cake Lissa was serving him would have to be his last because he and Clair had to get Willy home.

It helped Clair's attitude considerably to hear Jace include her, but she reminded herself that she was going to practice restraint when it came to him as they finally thanked Rennie for the meal and left.

"We're going to let Clair read our story tonight," Jace told Willy as they crossed the yards amid the first few flakes of snow to fall, just as the weatherman had predicted. "How 'bout she helps you on with your pajamas, too?"

"No," Willy answered unceremoniously. "No see me," he declared as he had in the past.

"He's very modest," Clair commented with a laugh.

"And stubborn, too," Jace added, ruffling the toddler's hair as they went inside.

Clair had the strangest sense at that moment that she was coming home, and it hit her so hard that it stopped her in her tracks in the entryway.

Very weird, she decided. And not at all helpful in maintaining that restraint she was working at. Nor was it helpful when she had a flash of the two of them putting Willy to bed for the night and then retiring themselves to Jace's bed like the married couple they suddenly seemed. To indulge in a night filled with the sensual benefits a married couple could so freely share.

But that wasn't going to happen, she lectured herself firmly, and she needed to stop her brain from torturing her with totally inappropriate fantasies.

"Give me about five minutes to get him into his pj's and then come on up," Jace advised as he ushered Willy upstairs.

Clair spent those five minutes reminding herself that she was only there for Willy's sake and that there was absolutely nothing—or at least there *should* be absolutely nothing—between her and Jace.

But as she finally climbed the stairs behind them and passed what she knew was Jace's bedroom, she still had a hot flash of unwanted desire that danced right up her spine.

Willy's door was open when she reached it, and she could see Jace snapping her nephew's pajamas bottoms to his pajama tops so she knew the coast was clear, but she knocked on the doorjamb, anyway.

"Come on in," Jace invited from where he sat on the edge of the mattress with Willy standing in the vee of his thighs.

Then to Willy he said, "What do you say you and Clair sit in the rocker tonight and I'll stay over here?"

"No. You hode me," Willy demanded.

"You'd be able to see the pictures a whole lot better if Clair holds you."

"No."

Jace gave her an I-tried shrug of his eyebrows as Willy ran for the rocking chair and dragged it to the bedside the moment Jace was finished fastening his pajamas.

"Sit, Unca Ace," Willy ordered and the two of them took up the same position they'd adopted since the first night Clair had been with them, leaving her to perch on the edge of the bed again, in the spot Jace had just abandoned.

Green Eggs and Ham was the evening's selection, and Clair put as much verve as she could into the reading, making sure that once she'd read the rhyme

on each page she held the book across the breach between bed and rocker for Willy to see the pictures.

He was snuggled against Jace's chest with his favorite reindeer washcloth, and he enjoyed the book—
smiling at the pictures and repeating words to Jace for
emphasis. Clair's being there and doing the reading
were only incidental, and Willy never responded directly to her, tuning her out as if she were just the
instrument delivering his entertainment, like the television set.

At the end of the story her nephew's eyelids were
heavy, and once again, by the time Jace had him situated under the covers and tucked in, the little boy
was sound asleep and didn't even know he was kissed
good-night by them both.

Then they tiptoed out of his room and down the
stairs.

"That was a lively rendition of *Green Eggs and
Ham*," Jace said as he led the way into the living
room, apparently just assuming she would stay awhile
tonight as she had the previous evening.

Not that Clair was unhappy with the assumption.
She'd been longing since the moment she'd left him
in the driveway late that afternoon for time alone with
him, and it was nice that she didn't have to trump up
an excuse to finally get that.

"Maybe you should give up your ad agency job and
go on the road as a storyteller," he added, teasing her
as he sat sideways on the sofa, bracing his cowboy-
booted foot on one knee while he rested the other knee

on the cushion and patted the spot just in front of it in invitation.

Clair didn't hesitate to accept the invitation. In fact, she unintentionally sat so close to him that his shin ran the length of her hip and thigh, sending a charge through her at that initial, innocent contact.

She couldn't move away without making it an issue, though, so she had to stay put. But she tried not to like it so much.

"I don't know," she said to his comment about going on the road as a storyteller. "I don't think it offers a very good benefits package. I'd probably better stick with the agency."

"And what exactly do you do there? You've never said."

"I'm an account executive. The youngest woman in the history of the company to be promoted that high."

"Pretty impressive. I'll bet that took no small number of hours, including plenty of overtime."

"Plenty," she confirmed. "I've worked six-day weeks almost every week since I started, and more nights and Sundays than I'd like to count. Sometimes it feels as though I live in my office and just pit-stop at my apartment. Plus I've only taken two weeks vacation in eight years."

"You must really like the work."

"I love it."

"I thought you might have been talkin' from your own perspective today when you were sayin' workin' might give my mother a feeling of usefulness and independence.''

"Definitely independence. Being able to get out on my own, not to have to rely on my father, was a big deal to me. A very big deal. It isn't easy to be dependent on someone who isn't dependable.''

"You say that as if your job is your lifeline.''

"I guess that's how I've always seen it.''

"Be hard to change it in any way then, I'd guess.''

Clair had the sense that he was doing to her what she'd done to him whenever the opportunity had presented itself—subtly making his own case in regards to who was better equipped to raise Willy without coming right out and saying it.

"I don't see any reason why I should have to change it,'' she said.

"Well, for instance, if you ever got married or had kids—those are things that cause changes in lifestyle.''

"I think I could adapt.''

Jace smiled as if he knew better. "I'll bet you don't even have a cat because it takes too much time you can't spare, and you probably bought a goldfish that died of neglect.''

"It was a fungus in the bowl,'' she defended before recalling that he was only guessing.

But this was definitely not something she wanted to get into with him so she tossed the conversational ball into his court. "What about you? Have you ever worked outside of ranching and farming?''

"Sure. I worked my way through college doing a lot of things that taught me I didn't like any job that cooped me up. Especially in an office. Sittin' behind a desk is my idea of hell.''

"What kinds of jobs did you have?''

"Telephone soliciting. Checkin' groceries. Book-keepin'. Clerkin' in an electrical supply company. Packin' meat. Then I tried tendin' bar and could stand that enough to stick with it until I graduated. But the day I had that degree in my hand I high-tailed it back here to do what I'd learned through experience was what I wanted to do.''

"Work on the family ranch,'' she concluded for him.

"Right. Now I do odd jobs to make a little extra money when I need it, but basically I'm a man of the land.''

"And you wouldn't want to change that,'' she countered pointedly.

Jace gave her a lopsided grin that awarded her match point. "No, I wouldn't.''

And apparently he didn't want to talk about that any more than she did because what he did change was the subject. "So does your bein' so devoted to your work mean you haven't had time for romance?''

"Romance? Who has time for romance these days?'' she joked.

"No romance?'' he said as if it were a crime against nature.

Clair couldn't resist smiling at the subtle compliment that she appreciated more than she wished she did.

"Well, I was engaged until just a little while ago.''

And she suffered a twinge of leftover pain that came with the memory.

"Engaged? That's somethin'," he said, his interest obviously piqued. "Who was the lucky man?"

"His name is Lyle White. He's a professor of philosophy at the university."

"A gentleman and a scholar?"

Clair gave a wry chuckle that lacked mirth. "I hadn't thought of him that way, but I guess so."

"How had you thought of him?"

"Mostly I've thought of him as the antithesis of my father."

Jace made a face and let out a grim chuckle. "That was his selling point? That he wasn't like your father? Doesn't sound like romance to me."

"No, I suppose it doesn't. And now that I think about it, there wasn't a lot of romance in the relationship. But Lyle is reliable and steady and stable, and in comparison to Dad, that had its appeal."

"You were swept off your feet by reliable, steady and stable?"

"There was no being swept off my feet," she said, thinking that more of that was going on with Jace than it ever had with Lyle White and wondering suddenly why she'd been so willing to accept the lack of it with Lyle.

"But you thought reliable, steady and stable was enough?"

"I guess I did."

"And then you wised up and got out?"

"Well, sort of."

"How sort of."

She couldn't tell him that the real catalyst to her breakup with Lyle had been when she'd told him she'd decided she wanted to raise Willy, and Lyle had said he didn't want his life disrupted by a child, that if she pursued her nephew, they were through. And she'd opted for being through.

But she could tell Jace what she'd realized about the relationship after the fact.

"I guess you could say I wised up when I looked back at things. That was when I saw just how stuck in his ways Lyle was. How intractable. How obstinate and inflexible. Among other things."

"Don't leave me hanging. Among what other things?"

Clair took a deep breath and sighed it out, feeling worse and worse the more they talked about Lyle, yet compelled to go on in spite of it. "The academic life can be pretty insular and within it Lyle is a big deal. He's widely published. He's respected and considered a great mind, a great thinker. That gives him a lot of status, and that status comes with some pretty big ego boosters. He's accustomed to having things his way and that's how he likes it. Even in our relationship everything had to revolve around him. I had to be the one to bend, to always give up what I wanted. He even insisted that I see my friends only when he wasn't around—like for weekday lunches or evenings when he was busy, because he didn't want to associate with them. He really didn't want to associate with anyone who didn't fawn all over him."

"And you finally got fed up?"

"For the most part I just did all the adapting to keep the peace," she admitted, embarrassed by the truth in it. "But I was starting to get fed up when he wanted me to give up my apartment and move in with him. He lived a block away from campus and I lived near my office. I suggested a compromise—that we move to a totally new place that was halfway between so we'd both have about the same commute. But there was no way he was doing that. And then, in the middle of that struggle, I learned about Kristin."

Clair ended on an ominous note and needed a moment to calm her own emotions before she could go on.

"He wasn't sympathetic?" Jace said in an understanding, compassionate voice.

"Worse. He said she deserved what she got and I should just close the book on that part of my life and be glad it was done with."

"And the idea of Willy?"

Clair had another, stronger sense that Jace knew why she was in Elk Creek. But she'd gone from feeling bad in the telling of this to feeling relieved to get it off her chest, so she said, "Lyle told me to just forget I'd ever found out about Willy. Nephew or not, I should just write him off. He said Willy would probably grow up to be no better than his mother, anyway, and at least I wouldn't have to be bothered with someone that ignorant a second time."

"Nice guy," Jace commented under his breath, raising his eyebrows at what Clair had just confided.

"I didn't realize just how *not* nice he was until that moment. I said what if I *wanted* to be 'bothered' with Willy. He said he didn't—that he absolutely refused to be. And in the end I decided that the expense of my adapting to him that far was just too high. I'd already given up more than I should have to be with him. I wasn't giving up Willy, too."

She half expected Jace to remind her that she didn't *have* Willy. Lyle had, after all.

But Jace didn't do that. He didn't seize the opportunity to address in any way what she'd alluded to without coming right out and saying it—that she wanted Willy, that she wanted to raise him herself.

Instead he said, "Still, it must have hurt you. If you were engaged to the man, you must have loved him."

"I loved him. But in retrospect I discovered that I didn't love him the way I should have loved him to marry him. What we were talking about before—the reliable, steady, stable, not-like-my-father stuff? I think that played a bigger part in my choosing Lyle than love or passion." Or the kind of desire she felt every minute she was with Jace....

"Then I think it was good you got out when you did."

"Me, too," she agreed, but in a voice so low it sounded wounded even to her.

"Do you really?" Jace asked, his denim-blue eyes probing hers as if for an answer.

"I really do," she said after considering it, able to add some conviction to her tone this time because she'd realized in that moment of thinking about it that she honestly did feel it was good that she got out of the relationship with Lyle.

"It hasn't been easy, I'll admit that," she said then. "Lyle was my philosophy professor the last semester of college—that's how we met—so we were together for a long time. And I'd accepted his ring, I was going to marry him. Since we broke up I've felt bad about it, but not devastated the way I would have if I'd been *in* love with him. In fact, I've felt almost relief, which tells me he wasn't right for me."

Jace nodded his head, slowly, thoughtfully, still searching her eyes, her expression. "But it hurts just the same," he nearly whispered.

Clair shrugged one shoulder weakly. "Yes," she conceded. "It especially hurt that he was so callous about Kristin. He was around before all this happened with her. He knew how close we were."

Jace reached over and took her hand, holding it as softly as if it were a butterfly, rubbing the back with a tender thumb. "You deserve better, Clair," he said. "Much, much better."

And although she hadn't thought that before, Jace's saying it made her believe it. It even made her smile. "I do," she agreed with some vigor.

A smile tugged at Jace's mouth, too, and as if that conclusion freed them of the somber subject, he got up from the couch suddenly and took her with him to the picture window.

"Here it comes," he said in a brighter tone, referring to the full-blown snow that was falling just beyond the porch.

Standing beside him, Clair watched the big, fat, fluffy flakes floating to the ground, and seeing the pure, crystalline glow of moonlight reflected off each one while being with Jace, having him hold her hand, was enough to make her feel a whole new sense of well-being.

"It's beautiful, isn't it?" she whispered, as if a louder voice might disturb it.

"Mmm."

He sounded so in awe that she just had to take her eyes away from the silent spectacle outside to glance up at his perfectly chiseled profile and see his appreciation herself. And she knew when she did that he'd been right about himself when he'd said he was a man of the land. He was. A man of the land and of all of nature. Elemental. Of the earth. Definitely not someone who would ever be happy cooped up in an office the way she was every day.

And despite the fact that they were so different—as different as night and day—he was very appealing to her. This rugged man who had been honed by working with his hands, by the outdoors. Who could be so gentle that his hand around hers was featherlight.

As if he felt her staring at him, he turned and again looked deeply into her eyes.

There was no artifice about him. No posturing. No need to be revered by other people, because he knew who and what he was and was comfortable with it. Confident in his own abilities. In himself. And seeing it made something in Clair's heart seem to open up.

To blossom. Something she didn't understand. Something she thought she should probably try to combat.

But it felt too nice to fight. At least for that moment. And instead she just let it fill her with warmth and wonder and a kind of joy she couldn't ever remember feeling before.

"So much for knowin' better," he said to himself as he placed his other hand along her cheek and leaned over enough to capture her lips with his.

That first kiss was so soft, so sweet, so chaste, that Clair was almost afraid it would be like the first kiss he'd ever given her and would end too soon.

Which it did.

But then he came back again. And again. Each time for a little longer. Each kiss a little deeper. Until he stayed. Until his lips parted and coaxed hers to part, too. Until mouths were suddenly open. And his tongue introduced itself to her, tentatively tracing the bare insides of her lips, the sharp edges of her teeth, then greeting her tongue, too.

By then his arms were around her and he was holding her pressed against him. His big hands were splayed out on her back, doing a massage she began to long for on other body parts. Other, much more sensitive, body parts.

By then her own arms were around him and she was delving into hard ridges of muscle and wishing to feel them without his shirt as chaperone.

Her nipples were hard knots making themselves known at his chest and yearning for some attention from those wonderful hands kneading her spine, working their way lower, to just the beginning swell of her derriere.

And if she'd had any lingering doubts about ending things with Lyle before, she certainly didn't have any as Jace's tongue did a circle dance with hers and increased the level of passion play with each orbit, with each meeting of tip to tip, with each stroke of tongue to tongue. Because never had Lyle brought to life the things that just a kiss from Jace brought to life in her. Never had Lyle made her feel what just a kiss from Jace made her feel. Never had she wanted Lyle the way she wanted Jace....

But when the reality of that sank in it scared her. And she remembered that she hadn't left Lyle behind to find Jace. She'd left Lyle behind to find Willy.

And kissing Jace—no matter how incredible it was and how much she wanted it to go on and on—was not aiding her cause.

So, even though she didn't want to, even though her whole body, her whole being, was crying out not to, she ended their kissing.

"I should go," she said in a low, breathless voice that nearly begged him not to let her.

"Mmm," he muttered for a second time, recapturing her lips with his and tempting her to forget her resolve.

"Really," she said between kisses that took first her lower lip between his and then her upper.

"Are you sure?" he asked, kissing one corner of her mouth, then the other, and nuzzling her cheek with his nose.

"I'm sure," she said even more breathlessly, less convinced, less convincing.

But then she thought of Willy again and said, "I'm really sure."

Apparently that was enough to let him know she meant it, because he took a deep breath, sighed it out and finally stood up too straight to kiss her again.

"Okay," he conceded reluctantly.

Then he slid his hands to her shoulders and down her arms until he was holding only her hands. He brought one of her hands to his mouth and kissed the back of it, lingering long enough to breathe a luxury of hot air there before he let go of that hand, too, and took her to the front door holding only the other one.

"Do you think we'll be snowed in tomorrow the way they're saying?" she asked, hating how enticing the idea was of lying before a roaring fire while drifts of snow piled up outside.

"I wouldn't be surprised," Jace said, his voice still deep and raspy. Then, after a moment of looking down at her intently, a smile playing on those wonderful lips, he seemed to slip out of the intimacy that had been between them and return to a just-friendly tone. "I was thinkin' about replacing the garbage disposal tomorrow. What would you say to bein' in charge of Willy while I'm at it? The space is too small for him to get into with me and since my head will be mostly inside the cabinet I won't be able to keep an eye on him."

"You mean I'd take care of him? On my own?"

"Well, you'd be takin' care of him here, and I'd be

available if you needed me. But basically on your own, yeah.''

''Will he let me do that, do you think?''

''It'll take some work but we'll just be firm with him.''

''Okay,'' Clair agreed, but her own insecurity echoed in her voice.

''If it doesn't work out we'll adjust,'' he assured her.

''But it would give me some one-on-one with him,'' she said, thinking out loud.

Jace didn't say anything to that, and she wondered if he was having second thoughts. So before he could rescind the offer, she said, ''I'd like that. I'd like to try it, anyway.''

''Then that's what we'll do. Why don't you come over about eleven? That'll give me a chance to do some snow shovelin' before I get started with the disposal.''

''I'll be here.''

Clair smiled up at him, thinking that this man had so many facets and no flaws that she could find even now.

He leaned around her and opened the front door, almost as if he had to or he might have whisked her in the other direction—up the stairs.

Or maybe that was only Clair's own wishful thinking.

''I'll see you in the morning, then,'' he said.

She nodded and tried to push away a sudden, intense longing for him to kiss her just once more the way he had at the window.

"Tell Rennie thanks again for dinner tonight."

"I will," Clair assured him as she finally felt him let go of her hand with one final squeeze.

"Good night," she murmured, stepping out into the cold night air.

"G'night."

Since she had refused to bring a coat, she headed in a hurry for the house next door, wrapping her arms around herself as protection from the frigid air.

But not even that shock of cold could wipe away thoughts of Jace. Yearnings for Jace. For more of what they'd just shared. And some of what she only wished they had.

And the whole way to Rennie Jennings's house Clair couldn't help wishing with all her being that the arms that were hugging her weren't her own.

And that the bed she was rushing to wasn't, either....

Chapter Seven

There were fifteen inches of snow on the ground by morning, and it was still falling so heavily that Clair couldn't see to the end of the block when she looked out her bedroom window.

However, she could see Jace and Willy shoveling the sidewalk that ran in front of Rennie's house, their house and the house on the other side of them. Just the way Rennie had told her Jace did whenever it snowed.

It was early yet, and Clair was still in her bathrobe, steaming coffee mug in hand. She was headed for the shower before too long, but while she sipped her coffee she couldn't think of another show she'd rather be watching or another thing she'd rather be doing, so she stayed where she was and enjoyed the sight.

She couldn't see much of Jace's face. He had on an old, salt-stained cowboy hat pulled low over his brow to keep the snow off his head, and he was looking down at what he was doing, doubly obscuring his handsome features. But it wasn't actually his face that she was interested in at that moment, anyway.

He had the shoveling down to a rhythm, so it was like watching a well-oiled machine or some kind of interpretive dance. Powerful legs braced his weight and that of the heavy shovelfuls of snow as his broad back bent to the task and muscular arms wielded the tool.

It was beauty in motion in its own fashion. Beauty clad in cowboys boots, faded jeans that caressed his thighs and rear end with a loving touch, a jean jacket that brushed his hips and encased his upper body as perfectly as any Armani suit, and shearling gloves that only added to the massiveness of hands that Clair craved the touch of.

No, that wasn't a good thing to think about, she reprimanded herself. That was a perilous frontier to venture into. All the more perilous because she wanted so much to venture into it.

But she knew she couldn't. In spite of how the previous three evenings had ended.

She hoped that spending today with Willy, being in charge of him and sort of having him to herself, would finally allow her to connect with him. And then maybe she could speed things up, let Jace know why she was really in Elk Creek and take her nephew back to Chicago with her before whatever was happening between her and Jace went any further. Because Willy was her goal, and she'd spent the last twelve hours trying to burn that into her brain so she wouldn't keep lapsing into things she shouldn't be lapsing into with Jace.

With that in mind, Clair forced her gaze off Jace and onto Willy. Her nephew worked with a plastic toy snow shovel behind the big man, copying his movements with the small amount of snow Jace left behind.

Willy was dressed much as Jace was except that his boots were snow boots and his coat was the heavy parka Clair had seen him wearing in the past. He wore jeans, gloves and a cowboy hat that made Clair smile. It was too big for him, so it fell all the way to his eyebrows and the tops of his ears.

But keeping her eyes off Jace was impossible, and before she knew it she was watching them both as they worked together. As Jace made sure to turn around after every few strokes to see what Willy was up to. As Jace paused to help Willy adjust his gloves and hat when they went askew. As Willy studied how Jace jabbed the shovel into the white stuff, lifted it and tossed it aside, then did the same thing himself. As Willy stopped when Jace stopped and brushed snow off himself just the way Jace did.

It was funny. But it was touching, too. And for the first time Clair wondered how it would be for the two of them to lose each other.

Oh, that wasn't a good thing to think about, either, she realized when it stabbed at her from the inside.

But Jace and Willy weren't family, she thought as she searched for some reason, some rationalization that would ease that ache. They hadn't even been an adopted family for very long. So maybe she wouldn't be doing any actual damage by breaking them up.

Breaking them up...

She didn't like the sound of that.

But that was what she'd be doing, and there was no spin she could put on it that wouldn't make it so. She just had to face it—she was going to hurt them both.

It wasn't easy to accept that. Hurting anyone was something she tried never to do.

But what was the alternative?

The alternative was to leave things as they were. To leave Willy to Jace.

Just then Willy's hat flew off and, as he looked up to see where it went, Clair caught such a clear glimpse of her sister in him that it made her catch her breath.

And in that moment she knew she just couldn't accept the alternative.

In that moment she was reminded all over again that Willy was Kristin's son. That he was Clair's nephew. That he was a Fletcher.

And whether or not Willy had bonded with her yet, Clair felt bonded to him. She felt bonded to him in a way that Jace could never be, no matter how good he was with him, no matter how much hero worship Willy had for Jace. None of that canceled out that deeper tie Clair had with the little boy. So how could she just turn her back on him, on all of that, walk away and leave him to Jace?

She couldn't. Not even if it caused some pain for everyone involved.

The pain would only be in the short run, she reasoned—again in an attempt to make herself feel better
about the whole thing.

And in the long run she truly believed that Willy
would be better off with his own family. That he
would be better off with someone who could keep his
mother alive for him. With someone who could let him
know his history, let him know who and where and
what he'd come from. That he would be better off with
someone who would keep him connected to his roots.

And Jace, too, would be better off if he were free
of raising a child who wasn't his, she told herself. If
he were free to go on with his life, to meet someone
and fall in love with her without the encumbrance of
someone else's child. Free to start a family of his own
from scratch.

In time everyone would be better off, and that was
what she had to keep in mind. She was only doing
what was right.

At least she *hoped* it was what was right.

No, it was. In the long run, it was.

Except that, as hard as Clair worked to believe that,
deep down she still felt bad.

Bad for Jace to be without Willy.

Bad for Willy to be without Jace.

And bad for herself, too.

Because when this was finally over and Jace was
free to go on with his life, she'd know that was just
what he was doing. She'd be left to picture him making that life with someone else.

And she suddenly knew without a doubt that that

would hurt her every bit as much as she was going to hurt him....

"Doan wanna pay wis Cair. Wanna hep you."

Willy's decree came in answer to Jace explaining that he needed to work alone today but that Willy got to play with Clair. As if it were a giant treat.

Willy didn't see it that way.

"We can do anything you want, Willy," Clair interjected.

"Wanna hep Unca Ace," came the logical answer, accompanied by a scowl in her direction that said, if the toddler could banish her from the planet, he would.

"You just can't today," Jace said firmly. "Now take Clair into your room and show her your toys."

"No."

"Willy..." Jace's tone was full of warning.

"I doan yike her. She's a gu-wl."

Clair tried not to let that hurt her feelings but it did.

"Hey, I don't want to hear that," Jace said sternly. "And since when don't you like girls? You liked Lissa just fine last night."

"*Big* gu-wls," Willy qualified.

"Big girls are the best kind," Jace said, barely suppressing a smile as he glanced up pointedly at Clair. "You're just being contrary now," he said. "If you're a good boy and you play nice with Clair while I work, we'll go out and build a snowman when I'm finished. The three of us. But if you aren't a good boy and you don't play nice with Clair, no snowman and no popcorn tonight with the *Toy Story* movie, either."

Clair didn't think it was possible but Willy's scowl got darker and deeper. And for the first time she thought he was actually mad at Jace.

It seemed like a moment she should seize. "Why don't you show me your favorite toy, Willy, and we'll play with it."

"Go on, now, boy. And be nice," Jace said with just enough force to let Willy know he meant business.

Willy spent another moment giving him the two-and-a-half-year-old version of the evil eye, then switched it to Clair, turned and stomped off.

Jace gave her a sympathetic smile. "Okay. You're on your own. Good luck."

"Thanks. I think I may need it."

There was no doubt about it, she definitely needed it.

No sooner had Clair followed Willy out of the kitchen, where Jace was opening his toolbox to get to work, than Clair found her nephew opening the front door and—without a coat on—charging outside as he announced he was "dunna time the twee."

"You can't go out there and climb the tree," she exclaimed, running after him.

She caught him just as he was about to go down the porch steps. "It's too cold out here. We have to play in the house," she told Willy as she took his hand and struggled to keep hold of it to pull him back into the house while he fought to get away.

"Now let's be nice, Willy," she said, attempting to sound like Jace in his authoritative mode. But it had absolutely no effect on Willy, and she finally had to pick him up and carry him inside.

Once she had, she locked the door so he couldn't run out again and took him upstairs to his room before she put him down.

"Now let's see… What should we do?" she said, surveying the possibilities among the toys that spilled out of a wooden toy box and lined shelves on two walls.

"I wanna hep Unca Ace."

"I know but you can't today. So let's you and I do something fun. How about that ball over there? Do you like to throw the ball?"

"You fo de ball. I wanna go down 'tairs."

And off he went, leaving Clair alone in his room before she knew he was going to run away again.

"Maybe I need more than luck," she said to herself.

She found Willy in the kitchen with Jace. Jace was on his back on the floor, his upper body inside the cabinet under the sink, his long, jean-clad legs bent at the knees. Willy was standing between them, reciting the "I wanna hep you" chant.

Down came Jace's arms from working on the disposal to lift the little boy out from between his tree-trunk thighs so he could slide out of the cupboard.

"He keeps getting away from me," Clair said, stating the obvious and hating the fact that frustration already sounded in her voice.

Jace nodded knowingly, and Clair wondered if what he knew was how hard it was to keep control of the headstrong two-year-old, or if what he knew was that she wouldn't be good at this.

But either way he was patient with them both.

"How 'bout a tent?" he suggested. "Snowy days are good days to make a tent."

"I make a great tent," Clair lied.

"And you can take your Digimon guys into the tent to play with."

Willy frowned at the idea but didn't reject it out of hand the way he usually did.

"Digimon?" Clair asked.

"They're these kind of animal-monster things. Pokémon's competition."

Clair wasn't sure she knew what Pokémon was, either, but she didn't want to seem stupid or uninformed, so she just acted as if she knew what he was talking about.

"I'd love to play with your Digimon stuff. And build a tent," she said with elaborate enthusiasm.

Willy looked at her as if she were nuts, but he actually conceded.

"You can take a sheet out of the upstairs closet to make the tent," Jace told her then.

"Should I build it in Willy's room or—"

Another smile eased its way onto Jace's breathtakingly handsome face as he seemed only then to see through her fib about being a great tent maker. "We like to do it in the living room. That way you can tuck one end of the sheet behind the sofa cushions, tie one of the other corners around a desk leg and the other one to the back of the rocker."

"Got it," Clair said, tearing her eyes off the appealing sight of the big man sitting on the floor, his wrists resting on his upraised knees, hands dangling over his shins as if he were perfectly comfortable down there.

"I'm sorry we bothered you," she apologized.

"No problem."

But he was beginning to sound skeptical. As if he wasn't sure she could actually handle Willy.

And even though she wasn't too sure of that herself, she decided to redouble her efforts to prove she could.

But as the day wore on it was no easy task.

The tent was a bust. While she rearranged the living room making the tent out of a sheet, Willy played with his Digimon toys. By the time she was finished and the tent was ready to occupy, he'd lost interest, found his toy tool belt and was once again in the kitchen with Jace.

Leaving the mess in the living room, Clair took her nephew upstairs again and this time managed to engage him in coloring the pages of a coloring book. Until he wandered away and scribbled on the wall while she was concentrating on staying in the lines.

Lunch was a fiasco.

She offered to make sandwiches and encouraged Willy to help her so Jace could go on working.

She and Jace were going to have ham and cheese sandwiches. Willy wanted peanut butter and jelly, and he wanted to make it himself. But rather than spread the peanut butter and jelly on the bread Clair set out in front of him, he smeared it up his arms.

Then he pitched a fit when she took him upstairs to wash him off because he wanted to *eat* the PB and J off, insisting that he didn't like it on "bwead." And in the process he smeared the stuff on Clair and much of the bathroom.

After lunch was no better.

Willy refused to work on the puzzle Clair tried to entice him with. He didn't want to hear her read him a story. He didn't want to build anything with his Lego. Neither the Matchbox cars or the Tonka trucks appealed to him. Talking Elmo tickled Clair's fancy but only sent Willy once more fleeing to the kitchen to be with Jace.

She began to wonder if her nephew was going out of his way to be contrary just to get her off his back. But she persevered regardless, determined to find some common ground between them and convince him she was as much fun to be with as Jace was.

"Are these your fish, Willy?" she asked on what seemed like the millionth trip to retrieve him from Jace's side.

The ten-gallon fish tank was in the den and could be seen from the doorway. Clair hadn't ventured in there yet today, but since the afternoon was drawing to a close and she still felt like a failure with the little boy, she was willing to try just about anything.

"Fish-uz?" Willy said, perking right up out of his pout over once again being kept from his Unca Ace.

Not suspicious at all, Clair thought she'd hit on a winner and carried him into the den.

"You like the fish-uz?" she asked.

"Down!" he demanded.

Clair complied, setting him on the den floor.

"Watch," he said, running to the desk with the first hint of genuine eagerness to show her something.

Clair was so thrilled that he was finally interacting with her, rather than trying to thwart her every attempt so he could get back to Jace, that she did as the two-year-old had told her to do and merely stood by and watched as he wrestled with the desk chair to roll it to the side of the tank.

It occurred to her that he wanted her to watch the fish, so after getting a kick out of the sight of him climbing onto the chair she turned her focus on the fish swimming peacefully in the tank.

"That's a pretty one—that bright yellow one with the black stripes," she said to show him that she liked them, too.

And even when, from the corner of her eye, she saw him lift the lid on the tank, all she thought was that he was going to feed them—a job she assumed Jace might have taught him.

But did Willy feed the fish?

Oh, no.

Before Clair realized what he was doing, he'd plunged his hand and arm—shirtsleeve and all—into the tank, splashing water everywhere. Then he actually managed to catch one of the fish, pulling it out of the tank only to lose the slippery thing and drop it on the floor.

"Oh, Willy!" Clair shrieked.

"I dit it," he assured her without the slightest alarm.

"No, no! You can't get it. You'll hurt it," Clair said, unsure what to do, knowing Willy was only going to compound the problem, and loath to pick up the slimy fish in her own bare hand.

"Is there a net or something?" she asked.

"I dit it," her nephew repeated, nearly stepping on the fish as he climbed off the chair. But he had less luck recapturing the fish than he'd had catching it in the first place as he splashed into the puddle of water where the fish wriggled wildly.

Then, when Willy finally did get hold of the fish, he grabbed it too forcefully and squirted it out of his hand again, right under the low-lying cabinet on which the tank sat.

Clair had no idea how long fish could live outside the water but she was certain it wasn't long. She knew she was going to have to just grab the thing to put it back in the tank, that she couldn't waste any more time.

Getting down on her hands and knees to look under the cabinet, she could barely see the fish where it had slid across the hardwood floor nearly to the baseboard.

"Dit it," Willy ordered her from where he'd dropped to all fours the same way she had, his cheek flat to the floor so he could see the fish, too.

Clair had to lie on her stomach, ignoring the puddled fish water she was soaking up with her shirt and slacks, so she could stretch her arm to its limits. But she finally reached the squirming, slimy fish, pulling her arm out in a hurry and leaping to her feet to toss it back into the tank as quickly as she could.

"Eew," she groaned, shuddering involuntarily at the whole experience just as she caught sight of Jace standing in the doorway.

She didn't know how long he'd been there but he was leaning a shoulder against the jamb, his arms crossed over his chest—as if he'd been there for some time.

Clair took an instant survey of her own drenched clothes, Willy's sopping-wet shirt, the water that seemed to be all over the place and the smell of fish that permeated the entire room, and just wanted to crawl into a hole.

Jace's expression was a combination of amusement and consternation as his gaze went from her to her nephew.

"What have I told you about this, Willy?" he said, aiming the consternation at the toddler.

Willy—who had gotten to his feet, too—shrugged hugely. "Sumpin'," he said as if whatever he'd been told escaped him at the moment.

"Yeah, something. You know better than to get the fish out of the tank."

"Cair wanna'd a see 'im."

So even at two and a half he knew how to pass the buck, Clair thought.

But she didn't mind. Rather than take umbrage she reveled in the fact that Willy was referring to her as a cohort.

"I'm sure Clair only wanted to see the fish in the

tank. Not out on the floor," Jace continued. "You *never* put your hand in the water or take the fish out of the water."

"Betuz de die," Willy finished for him, obviously recalling what he'd been told before, after all.

"Yes, because they die. And you don't like it when we have to flush them, do you?"

"No. Den I hafta cwy."

"That's right, it makes you cry. And we don't want them to die and you to have to cry."

"Can I hep you now?" the little boy asked suddenly, as if his latest naughty deed might finally reward him with being allowed in Jace's company.

"No, you can't *hep* me now. I'm all done," Jace said. Then, after another glance at the mess in the den and over his shoulder at the tent mess still in the living room, he added, "And apparently none too soon."

That news brightened Willy's entire outlook. "Can we go ou-side and make de snowman?"

"You know what? I don't think so. That was what we were going to do if you were good for Clair today. But you didn't do much behavin', did you?"

Willy's bottom lip came out. "No," he conceded in a grumble.

"So I guess we just have to get you into some dry clothes, go out and shovel again, and then come in without makin' a snowman, don't we?"

Willy gave Jace the dark, under-the-brows scowl again, but he didn't say anything.

"Go on up to your room and get out of those wet

clothes. I'll be up to get you some dry ones in a minute."

"I do it myself," Willy muttered as he walked off, hanging his head dejectedly and unknowingly tugging at Clair's heartstrings.

"Maybe he shouldn't be punished for today. Maybe it was my fault," she whispered so the retreating Willy couldn't hear.

Jace just shook his head. "Even little kids need not to be rewarded for breaking rules, Clair. Willy and I made a deal this morning—if he cooperated with you, we could make a snowman. He didn't do any cooperatin' that I saw, so no snowman."

"He still got to go to the park even after misbehaving at the doctor's office," she just had to point out.

Jace smiled. "Okay, so I let him slide a little. But the doctor's office wasn't a whole day of misbehavin'."

"He was so sad, though."

"Don't worry about it. He'll be happy again by the time you get back from changin' *your clothes*," Jace said, poking his sculptured chin in the direction of her soaked shirt and slacks to remind her of her own soiled condition.

"I do need to change," she conceded with a glance down at herself. "Just the smell is starting to make me sick—peanut butter, jelly and fish water."

He looked as if he might be about to laugh but refrained. "Why don't you go ahead to Rennie's and do that then. I'll clean up here."

Clair felt guilty for leaving him with the water that

dripped down the side of the fish tank and the cabinet it stood on into the slop already on the floor. But the smell her clothes were giving off really was beginning to get to her.

"Okay, but leave the messes in Willy's room and the living room. I'll pick those up as soon as I get back."

Jace didn't look convinced but he said, "You can do that while I fix supper and then maybe we can get the tiny terror to sit still for the movie so we can have a peaceful evening."

After the day she'd just put in, that was an appealing thought. Especially appealing because they'd be a threesome again.

"A peaceful evening sounds nice," she said, wishing her voice hadn't had such an intimate intonation. She amended it and added, "Willy gets popcorn, doesn't he? He didn't lose that, too?"

"No, he didn't lose that, too. One punishment is enough."

She was glad to hear that, glad to know Jace would be fair.

She was also glad to be standing there with him, alone for the first time all day, basking in the warm glow of his denim-blue eyes....

But that wasn't what she was supposed to be doing, and so she took a deep, steeling breath and said, "I'd better go get these clothes off."

She hadn't intended for that to sound intimate, either, but that's how it had come out. And Jace had heard it, too, because he smiled a crooked, one-sided smile.

"Yeah, I think you'd better," he agreed with an innuendo-laden tone of his own.

He could have been taking in nothing more than the sight of the peanut butter on the front of her clothes but having his gaze just in that general vicinity was enough to tighten her nipples.

"Oh, yeah, I'd better get going," she murmured to herself. Then more loudly she added, "I'll be back shortly."

"I'll be here," he said with a note of promise that answered that same thing in her voice.

It was on the tip of Clair's tongue to say that Willy wasn't the only one misbehaving today, that the two of them had no business flirting like this.

But she didn't. Instead she just left, hurrying through the falling snow to the house next door, all the while trying to tamp down the excitement induced by the idea of the evening to come.

Excitement she knew she shouldn't be entertaining and the pure, raw desire that came along with it.

Chapter Eight

Clair showered at warp speed to rid herself of the smells she'd come home with, reapplied blush and mascara, then chose a pair of black leggings and a beige, ribbon-yarn boat-neck tunic sweater to change into.

But when she realized just which sweater she'd pulled out of her suitcase she had second thoughts.

It was a sweater she never wore with a bra because the boat neck was wide and showed the straps. And she wasn't sure going braless was a good idea since she would be with Jace.

But the ribbon yarn was soft and warm and comfortable—the perfect thing for a snowbound night of watching a movie and eating popcorn.

Would being braless be all that noticeable? she asked herself.

Ordinarily she didn't think it was a problem. She was small-breasted enough to get away with it.

But ordinarily she wasn't with Jace.

What if he noticed and thought it was some kind of come-on? Especially after that little verbal dance they'd done as she was leaving today.

She didn't want him to think she was coming on to him. Because she wasn't. In fact, that was the last thing she was doing. At least intentionally. But she really wanted to wear that sweater.

She pulled it on over her head and studied her reflection in the bathroom mirror to get a better idea of how it might appear through his eyes. From the front and from the side.

Jace probably wouldn't even be able to tell, she decided. And if she were in Chicago, watching a video tape at home on a Saturday night, she would definitely not hesitate to wear it. So why couldn't she wear it tonight?

She decided there was no reason not to, and she left it on, feeling almost defiant, as if someone were trying to control what she could and couldn't wear and she was thwarting that control. She dressed for herself, she thought, not for anyone else.

Then she took out the clips that had held her hair all day and fluffed it into a free mass of curls, even pulling one as far over her right eye as it would go.

But once she had, she stopped short and took another long look at herself.

The curl pulled down over her eye was something

she would have done for a romantic evening out with Lyle. The curl was sexy.

And maybe that was going too far. After all, the sweater exposed almost all of her collarbones and a fair share of her shoulders, and with the curl falling down her forehead? Maybe it was too much.

So, change one or the other, she told herself.

But she just didn't want to.

She'd had a day of chasing a two-year-old, a day full of frustration that had seen Jace ushering her out of his house looking every bit as frazzled as she'd felt. She wanted to go back looking—and feeling—better. Looking and feeling as if the day hadn't taken any real toll on her. As if it hadn't gotten the better of her. And both the sweater and the sexy little curl accomplished that.

There wasn't any more to it. There really wasn't.

It wasn't a come-on. It wasn't a signal that she thought she was in line for a romantic evening or for a passionate ending to a romantic evening.

It was just a comfortable sweater and a curl, and there wasn't any more to it than that, she thought as the defiance made a resurgence.

Besides, she and Jace were two adults, not two teenagers who couldn't control themselves if one of them was braless and showing a little collarbone and a come-hither curl. So it shouldn't be any big deal, and she was keeping on the sweater and leaving the curl. Period.

With her heels dug in on the matter, she applied a light lipstick and spun away from the mirror as if to escape before she talked herself into either a more frumpy hairdo or more conservative clothes. Then she shrugged into her coat and headed back to Jace and Willy.

They were just going in from shoveling the walks again when she got there, and as Jace took off his coat she noticed that he'd changed clothes, too.

Of course, there was no way of knowing whether he'd gone without underwear the way she had and she gave herself a stern lecture for even entertaining such a thought. But he had replaced his work jeans with a fresh pair and put on a navy-blue plaid flannel shirt that looked so soft she was tempted to reach out and touch it.

Not that she did. Or would. But she did tell herself that his shirt justified her sweater because clearly he'd chosen something soft and warm and comfortable, too.

Dinner was a much calmer affair than lunch had been, with Jace back at the helm. He'd been right about Willy, who was over his mad and back to being intent on mimicking Jace's every movement again.

There was a slight difference in Willy's attitude toward Clair, though. He seemed more accepting of her being with them. He even included her to a small extent. And she thought that any amount of mess, frustration and frazzle was worth that.

Then came movie time, and after Jace had built a roaring fire in the fireplace, Willy settled onto the sofa between Jace and Clair to watch in rapt silence and eat popcorn.

That was where the three of them stayed right up

to the end of the film, when her nephew fell sound asleep with his head against Jace's arm.

"I'll just carry him up to bed. He won't wake up," Jace told her when they realized Willy was out like a light.

Clair nodded and watched as the big man gently scooped up the toddler, cradling him against his massive chest in a way that gave her a rush of warmth so intense her eyes followed them until they were completely out of sight.

But the moment they were, her gaze caught on the pile of debris left over from her afternoon's tent making, reminding her that she had one more mess to clean up.

She'd straightened Willy's bedroom while Jace was getting dinner ready but hadn't had the time to do the living room, too. They'd merely pushed aside the sheet and toys left over from that portion of the day's activities. But now that she had the chance, she opted for finally putting the living room back in order, including clearing away the popcorn and turning off the television and the VCR so the place was completely clean.

She'd just finished folding the sheet and left it and the Digimon monsters on the rocking chair when Jace came back.

"All tucked in?" she asked.

"All tucked in," he confirmed. Then he glanced around the room and added, "Thanks for cleaning up."

"It's the least I could do since I made most of the mess."

He had the good grace to smile without comment. Instead he said, "What do you say we sit in front of the fire and enjoy it before it burns itself out?"

"I wouldn't want to waste it," she agreed without a second thought.

Jace took cushions off the couch and positioned them on the floor so they could sit on one and rest their backs against the other. Or at least Clair could rest her back against the upended one. Jace sat at an angle with his side against it and his arm running along the edge, close enough behind her head that she could feel as much heat coming from his big body as she could from the fire.

When they were situated, she caught him glancing at the things on the rocker, and she thought she knew what he was thinking.

"I know. I really tore up the place today, didn't I?"

Jace's smile was impish. "I've seen tornadoes do less damage," he teased.

"It's your fault, you know."

"How is it my fault?" he asked with mock affront.

"You handle Willy so smoothly that you make it look easy. But it isn't easy." It was anything but. "I have to admit I ended up feeling pretty inadequate."

"Not everyone is cut out for parenting," he answered offhandedly.

But it made her slightly sorry that she'd admitted anything to him. "I don't think I did *that* bad," she countered even though she knew it wasn't true.

"I wasn't talking about you, so much."

She didn't believe him, but she played along, anyway. "Who else do you know who isn't cut out to be a parent?"

"My ex-wife, for one."

The subject of anyone not being cut out to be a parent struck too close to home, but Clair was so curious about his past that she couldn't resist opening the door if he was unlocking it.

"I know you mentioned that you were married," she said to encourage him to go on.

"For nearly five years," he confirmed.

"And she didn't want kids?" Clair couldn't imagine a relationship with Jace *not* including children. She'd never met a man so good with them.

"Stephanie—that's her name—said she wanted kids. At least, she said it before she decided to go to law school. We had our whole life mapped out together—college, marriage, a big family we'd raise here in Elk Creek—that's what we *both* said we wanted. But when it came time to put the big-family part into the picture, Stephanie had changed her mind. And lost whatever drive or instincts she might have had for it before."

Clair hoped he didn't think the same of her.

"I take it she was from around here?" she asked.

"Born and raised. We were sweethearts from kindergarten on. We went off to college together and got engaged just before I came back here and she went on to law school. We set the date for the week after she graduated, which was exactly when we got married."

Clair raised her eyebrows. "You were together from kindergarten?"

"There were some strayings along the way—hers and mine. I don't think we'd have been normal teenagers if we hadn't discovered attractions to other people here and there. But besides a few minor separations, yes, we were basically together from kindergarten on."

"Even with the separations it all sounds very neat and tidy." And not like a story that would have a divorce at the end of it.

"I thought it *was* all neat and tidy. But the first problem was that law school changed her and she wasn't happy in Elk Creek once she got back."

"She liked it here before that?"

"As much as I did. But when she came home with her law degree she started to say she thought the town was stifling. She started to talk about moving to a big city, somewhere she could make a name for herself as a high-powered attorney."

"Oh-oh."

"Yeah. She thought I should try to get a job with the state agriculture department and then we could both have careers somewhere away from here. 'Course I didn't want anything to do with that. I wanted to be here. Wanted to start a family and raise it here just the way we'd talked about."

"It must have been a rocky five years of marriage under those circumstances."

"It definitely wasn't smooth. Mostly it was a tug-of-war. Subtly, but a tug-of-war just the same. She was tryin' to get across to me how important her career was—which was such a change in her that I had a hard time seein' it—and I was tryin' to convince her she wanted to be a mother.''

''How were you doing that?''

''First by talkin' about it all the time. Pointin' out how cute and fun other people's kids were. Lettin' her know how strong my feelings about bein' a father were. Then I had a three stage plan—fish, puppy, baby.''

''Fish, puppy, baby?'' Clair repeated, barely suppressing a smile.

Jace did smile at it. ''I know. It sounds funny. But I figured I'd ease her into those maternal instincts. I couldn't believe she didn't have any. I thought I'd start out with fish—they're easy to take care of, decorative, calming. They only call for a little responsibility, a little plannin' for, a little scheduling. Then once she got involved in them, I'd bring home a puppy—a little more responsibility, a little more work, but who can resist 'em?''

''And from there you thought she'd decide she wanted a baby,'' Clair concluded for him.

''Right.''

''I've seen the fish but I haven't seen a dog around here.''

Jace's confirming chuckle was wry. ''Because we didn't get beyond the fish.''

''She let them die of neglect?'' Clair asked, recalling Jace accusing her of that and realizing only now that he'd probably been talking from his own experience with his ex-wife.

"She would have. I took care of them so that didn't happen. But she did see through my plan."

"And she didn't think it was a good one."

"She wanted her career at full blast. She'd worked hard to get her degree, to pass the bar. She wanted to keep her focus on her work. She didn't want to just be doin' the penny-ante legal things around here as a sideline to havin' kids."

"It does make sense," Clair admitted, understanding the other woman's attitude because her own career was so important to her.

"Yeah, I suppose it does. But livin' a childless, high-powered, fast-paced, two-career-couple life in a big city was as much my idea of hell as staying here got to be hers."

"And that was the death knell of the marriage."

Jace nodded, his expression somber. "The harder I pushed for what I wanted, the more determined she was to get out of Elk Creek. Finally we had to agree to go our separate ways."

"And this was even before you ended up with Willy?"

"Right. Stephanie would definitely not have been happy about that turn of events. In fact, if she hadn't left before, she would have then. She just came to the conclusion that she couldn't have the kind of career she wanted and kids, too."

Clair was reasonably sure that was the same conclusion he'd come to about her, and she felt as if she couldn't let it slide.

"If a person really wants both, they can do it," she said with more certainty than she felt.

She could see the skepticism on Jace's oh-so-handsome face and she knew that, after the day's exhibition of just how incompetent she was at the mothering part, she'd confirmed his doubts. She'd probably actually given him more doubts than he'd had before. And she expected him to say something along those lines.

But he didn't. Instead he said, "I suppose some people can do it all."

Clair didn't want to push the issue any further and tempt him to say more, so she accepted that tiny victory and said, "It must have been a terrible blow to end up divorced from someone you'd been with since childhood."

"It wasn't easy. The five years of tug-of-war went a long way in tearin' us apart, but there was still some grieving for what was lost. For what would never be."

The solemnity in his voice made Clair pause a moment before she said, "And now?"

He smiled again. Only slightly. Sadly. But as if to let her know that although he had vivid memories of the pain of his divorce that's all they were—memories.

"I'm over it. Over her," he said then, as his denim-blue eyes delved into hers. "In fact, lately I've been surprised by just how over it—and her—I am," he added pointedly.

"Oh? Just how over it—and her—are you?"

"Over it enough to be thinkin' about someone else.

All the time. Over it enough to be wantin' someone else...."

He caressed the side of her face with his free hand.

"Tonight, for instance," he said quietly, his voice no more than a whisper. "You look so terrific I haven't been able to think about anything else."

If Clair had thought that single curl over her eye was sexy, it was nothing compared to the sound of Jace's voice. Nothing compared to having his gorgeous, masculine face so close. Nothing compared to the woodsy scent of his aftershave or the look in his blue eyes that said he was enthralled by her.

And it was certainly nothing compared to the feel of that big, leathery hand on her face....

"This, in particular, has been driving me crazy all night," he confided as he kissed the very tip of her collarbone where it was exposed by the boat neck of her sweater.

Tiny, glimmering flecks of gold seemed to rain from that spot outward and all through her at that first touch of tender lips to her bare skin. And without considering whether it was wise or not, she tilted her head to allow him freer access.

He took it, too, kissing the sharp ridge of her collarbone to her shoulder where the sweater's neckline reconnected.

And in that moment Clair forgot what they'd been talking about. She forgot the allusions he'd made to the fact that she might not be cut out to be a mother. She forgot everything but how much she'd been wanting him to do just what he was doing.

The hand that cradled her face guided it toward him. At the same time he leaned forward and captured her mouth with his. Not that she wouldn't have willingly complied, because she would have. Something about being with him wiped away all reason in her, all sense, all thought of why she shouldn't be doing what she was doing, and left raw, naked desire underneath—the raw, naked desire that seemed to have been there beneath the surface since the first instant she'd set eyes on him.

She didn't understand it. She'd never experienced anything quite like it before. And maybe that was why it was so potent.

But whatever the cause, it *was* potent. Incredibly potent. So potent that it wiped away her ability to resist his appeal, to resist her own desires even when she knew, somewhere in her clouded mind, that she should.

Instead she just kissed him in return. She let her head fall back, she reached a hand to the side of his thickly corded neck and she kissed him every bit as intensely as he was kissing her.

She let her lips part in answer to his. She met his tongue with her own, when it came to play. And when his arms went around her and pulled her close, she went eagerly, taking a deep breath so the hardened knots of her nipples could brush the steel of his chest.

The man could kiss like no one she'd ever known. Hot and hard and insistent one minute, soft and light and teasing the next. Drawing her out of herself, so totally involving her that she lost herself in kissing him, lost all thought of anything but wanting him to go on kissing her. Wanting him to go on holding her. Wanting him to do more than kissing and holding....

Her own arms were completely around him then, and she filled her hands with muscles that seemed to have no end. With shoulders so broad she could barely span them.

His shirt was as soft as it had looked to be—new flannel over solid rock. But even as soft as it was, all Clair could think about was how much she wanted it out of her way. How much she wanted to feel his skin unhampered.

Their kisses were more serious by then. Deeper. Hungry. Almost urgent. And that almost urgency was sweeping through her to other spots as well. To hands that ached to be exploring bare flesh. To breasts that cried out to be touched. To other, more intimate spots that were dangerous to think about.

The craving grew and grew until she had to do something about it. Something that would let him know what was coursing through her. A craving that grew big enough to make her more bold.

So while he kneaded her back, her arms, her shoulders on top of her sweater, she pulled his shirttails from his jeans and took the dive under the flannel to his bare back.

The sound that rumbled from his throat let her know she'd done the right thing. That the touch of her hands on those satin-on-steel muscles of his back was as good for him as it was for her.

And it was good for her. Jace had a body that was

wonderful to look at in his clothes, and even more wonderful to the feel of her hands.

Clair reveled in it. She learned her way around every muscle, every tendon. And she enjoyed it all. It was just that she wanted to feel his touch on her bare skin, too.

Her nipples were so tight they ached, and she arched her back to convey the need they had for his attention, pressing them into his chest in what seemed like a screaming demand.

But she had the sense that he knew exactly what he was doing. Exactly how long to keep her wanting so the desire was heightened, so that when he finally slipped his hand under her sweater—just to her back— it was enough to drive her to a frenzy. A frenzy that caused her to dig her fingers into the unyielding strength of his shoulders, his biceps.

She felt him smile slightly as his tongue turned coy and toyed with hers. As his hands made an excruciatingly slow voyage up and down her spine before one of them continued to her side. To her stomach. Then upward to just the beginning swell of her breast.

Once more she arched her back and finally—*finally!*—he took the fullness of that yearning globe into his palm.

Oh, it felt so good!

She couldn't help the tiny moan that echoed from somewhere deep inside her. She couldn't help sitting up straighter and pushing her breast even more deeply into his hand. She couldn't help the course her own hands took around to *his* front, to pectorals she longed to see bared to the fire's glow, to have pressed to her own naked flesh. Her own naked flesh where his fabulous hand kneaded and caressed, where fingertips lightly circled the ultrasensitive nipple that kerneled into a pebble and strained for more, which he granted in gently pinching, pulling, tugging, teasing strokes.

She was falling ever deeper under the spell of a primitive sensuality that he was awakening within her, and she didn't care. She didn't care about anything but the feel of his hands on her. The feel of her hands on him, and the glittering gold desire for more.

But she didn't get more.

Just as her head fell back from his seeking, open mouth and he began to press delicate kisses down the column of her throat, just as she thought he was going to raise her sweater and let his mouth replace his hand on her breast, he stopped instead.

He stopped kissing her at all. He stopped touching her and pulled his hands completely out from under her clothes, settling into simply holding her. Closely. Tenderly. Almost absorbing her into himself. But nothing more.

"I don't know if it's smart to take this any further," he said in a voice so raspy, so husky with raw, unsatiated hunger that it revealed how difficult it was for him to stop.

Clair wanted to say that he didn't have to stop. That, in fact, she wanted him to take her upstairs to his bedroom and make love to her. That she'd never in her life wanted anything more than she wanted that at this moment.

But she didn't say any of it.

Because she knew he was right. She knew it wasn't smart to take this any further. And even though she also knew that it wouldn't take much encouragement on her part to get things started up again, she shouldn't do it. She couldn't do it. Not now that he'd given her a moment to recall all the reasons why it wasn't a good idea—to recall why she was there in the first place and what she was determined to accomplish. To remember that Willy was her real focus here....

"You're right," she managed to say, her own voice almost as raw with passion as his. "It's that *Toy Story* movie," she added, joking to make light of what didn't feel that way at all. "I understand it affects everyone like this."

Jace smiled down at her and laid his forehead on hers. "We'll have to watch something tamer next time," he said to play along. "Although I imagine that the *Power Rangers* and the *Smurfs* can be pretty hot, too."

"Oh, I'm sure," she agreed with a somewhat pained chuckle.

For a while they just remained the way they were—holding each other, brow to brow. And for Clair it helped to know that Jace wasn't any more anxious than she was to separate, despite the fact that he'd been the one to end what might have taken them all the way to making love if it had been left to her.

But they couldn't stay like that forever and, after a few more minutes of giving herself over to the warmth of his big body against hers, she said, "I'd better get home."

Jace didn't argue. But he also didn't let go of her. At least not immediately. And when he did, it was with a sigh that sounded resolved but reluctant.

Then he stood and held out a hand to help her up.

Clair slipped hers into it, feeling a familiarity so strong it was as if they'd been carved from the same stone.

Jace walked her to the door, still holding her hand, but not saying anything until he'd helped her on with her coat.

"Church tomorrow?" he asked.

"Church?" Clair parroted as if it were a foreign concept.

"Every Sunday. My mother would skin me alive if I didn't show up. But that doesn't mean you're obliged to go. I just thought—"

Clair didn't hear much of the rest of what he was saying as the idea of going to church with him sank in. It wasn't as if she was against organized religion. She'd attended services every Sunday herself growing up. But like so many things, in the fast pace of her adult life, churchgoing wasn't something she'd kept up.

But now that she was faced with the fact that the spiritual was yet another dimension Jace offered in Willy's upbringing that she hadn't so much as thought about, she couldn't just ignore it.

"In the morning? What time?" she asked, not as if

her going were dependent upon it but as confirmation that she'd go.

"All the denominations share the church building. Our service is at nine."

"And we'd be going together? The three of us, I mean—Willy goes, too?" she qualified, when the first part of that had sounded too much as though she were referring only to herself and Jace.

"Absolutely. Then there's Sunday dinner out at the ranch. You can meet my mother and brothers."

He said that so easily. As if it were no big deal. Lyle had had strict rules about when a woman was allowed to meet any of his relatives and would never have let it happen so soon.

"Church and a Sunday dinner with your family would be nice," Clair said, meaning it, because she actually did appreciate being included.

Jace was looking down at her, into her eyes, and for a moment she lost touch with things again and very nearly leaned into him so he could take her in his arms once more.

But she caught herself, tore her gaze away and instead opened the door.

Before she got through it Jace said, "Clair?"

She glanced up at him, her heart skipping a beat at how handsome he was, at how much she wanted to be back in his arms.

He laid one of those wonderful hands of his along the side of her face the way he had just before he'd kissed her for the first time tonight, bent forward and kissed her again. Softly. Sweetly. And yet with the full force of the passion they'd just cut short still lurking around the edges.

But then it was over, and all Clair could do was force herself out that front door into the cold of the snowy evening.

She hardly felt the chill though, as she walked along the white-powdered sidewalk to Rennie's house.

Because what she felt was the lingering heat of Jace's kiss, of Jace's arms, of Jace's touch.

And the nearly overwhelming drive to feel it again.

Chapter Nine

The only way Willy would sit still through Sunday church services was if Jace held him on his lap. But the next morning it was Jace who felt antsy as he juggled the toddler, Willy's favorite picture book and some munchies to keep the little boy occupied and quiet.

Jace had too much pent-up energy. Sexual energy. And having Clair sitting beside him, their legs and arms and sides coming into contact, even accidentally, wasn't helping.

Of course, he hadn't been able to find anything that *did* help since she'd left the night before. Not snow shoveling without a coat on. Not the two cold showers he'd taken. Not push-ups or sit-ups or arm curls. Not lecturing himself or reminding himself why he should be steering clear of her. Not telling himself he was a damn fool. And not even trying to concentrate on the sermon.

The plain truth of the matter was that he wanted Clair. He wanted her in the worst way. And now that the tap had been turned on, he couldn't seem to turn it off.

Stopping himself from making love to her the previous evening had been very difficult. It had taken recalling their conversation about Stephanie, starting to think about how much Clair was like Stephanie when it came to her career, and then topping it all off with his suspicions that Clair was in Elk Creek to take Willy away from him, before he'd been able to revive his willpower and put on the brakes.

But putting on the brakes had been completely on the surface. Below the surface, wanting her had gone on full force.

Everything that had come to mind to stop him the night before was true, though, and he needed to remember that. He needed to imprint it on his brain and maybe then these burning desires for her would calm down. He needed to face up to how much Clair was like Stephanie after law school and how she might be a threat to his raising Willy. He just didn't know why it was so damn hard to keep the negatives in the forefront of his mind.

Just look at her, a voice in the back of his head said in answer to that.

Okay, it was no wonder it was hard to keep the negatives in mind when there she was with that alabaster skin and that soft, curly hair that he now knew felt as silky as he'd thought it might.

There she sat with those Cupie-doll lips that tasted sweeter than any he'd ever tried, and those eyes—those big, pale-green eyes that looked like sparkling spring water.

There she sat with that compact little body encased in a brown knit dress that followed every perfect curve from its round neckline to her narrow hips where it fell to those slim ankles he had fantasies about kissing.

There she sat, and he was mush inside just looking at her from the corner of his eye....

Oh, yeah, it was no wonder he couldn't keep the negatives in mind.

Then something else occurred to him for the first time with quite a jolt. If Clair was like Stephanie when it came to career and lifestyle, maybe she was like Stephanie when it came to kids, too. And if that was the case, maybe she *hadn't* come to Elk Creek to take Willy away from him.

Okay, sure, she had made a comment here and there that had him thinking she was there to get custody of her nephew. But what if he was just being paranoid? After all, she'd also let him know that her career was important to her and that she worked six days a week. So, realistically, why would she *want* to add a two-year-old to that mix? Stephanie wouldn't have. Stephanie hadn't even wanted her own kids, let alone someone else's.

The logic in that seemed strong. It seemed reasonable. And if that were the case, if, like Stephanie, Clair didn't have room in her life for a child and hadn't come for Willy, could he relax with her? Could he relax all the way around with her, not just on the issue of Willy?

It seemed as though he could, because just thinking about not having to worry that Clair would try to take Willy made him feel instantly better. It made him feel more free.

More free to let himself go a little when it came to Clair and what was happening between them.

Because if Willy wasn't at risk, then the only thing at risk was Jace himself.

And if that was the case, he just might be willing to take that risk. Especially if it let him have what he wanted so much.

But was it true that Clair didn't want Willy?

He couldn't be absolutely positive. She hadn't said anything overtly about it in all the time she'd been in Elk Creek. Plus it wasn't as if Clair had a rapport with kids. Not with Willy or with Rennie's niece. So maybe she honestly wasn't any more of a kid person than Stephanie had been.

Maybe Clair actually was only in Elk Creek to do what she'd said she was there to do—to meet and connect with her nephew. Nothing more than that. Just to establish a relationship that would be sustained through phone calls, the occasional visit and nothing else.

The more Jace thought about it, the more possible it seemed. The more likely it seemed.

Which meant that maybe he could relax. Maybe he

could let down his guard— well, as much of his guard as he'd been able to keep up. Maybe he could let down his guard and just roll with things. Just let things take their course.

And afterward, when Clair high-tailed it back to Chicago, what then? he asked himself.

He didn't want to think about that. At least, he didn't want to think about it beyond thinking that maybe he could just deal with it when the time came.

Because right at that moment he just wanted some relief. Relief from the stress and worry and fight to keep under control what wouldn't be controlled—his attraction to Clair.

Besides, it was Sunday and Sunday was a day of rest, he reasoned. And even if that reasoning was flimsy, at that moment it seemed like enough.

Sure he'd have to face up to things he might not want to face up to down the road—like Clair leaving—but today he could put everything on hold.

Oh, that was an appealing proposition!

Too appealing not to grab on to and put into action....

He took a deep breath and sighed it out, letting a new sense of peace settle over him.

Yep, that's what he was going to do. He was going to give in, enjoy Clair for the time being and forget everything else.

A few of the minister's words pulled Jace out of his reverie, and he was ashamed of himself for sitting in church thinking what he was thinking.

But shame or no shame, it didn't really matter when

Willy dropped his book. Jace leaned over to pick it up and got a glimpse of Clair's legs where they peeked out from under the hem of her skirt.

Oh man, did he want her...

And maybe wanting her was what was doing his thinking for him.

But even as that idea flashed through his mind, he knew it wasn't totally true, because wanting Clair wasn't all he felt about her. She might be easier to resist if that were the way things were.

But the truth was, he had fun with her. He liked talking to her. He liked sharing even simple things with her, like tucking Willy in for the night. He just plain liked being around her. And whenever he was with her he felt better than he'd felt in a long time. In a long, long time.

And that wasn't anything to ignore. In fact, it felt like someone had given him a gift. A temporary gift, but a gift nevertheless. A gift he shouldn't deny himself. Certainly a gift he didn't want to deny himself.

And maybe whatever came of it was less important than the pleasure he was finding with her right now, in the present.

Besides, he realized as he thought about it, whether or not they let things between them go further than they already had, if she were to leave in the next hour he'd have pangs, he wouldn't be crazy about her going, and he'd miss her when she was gone.

So what was he sparing himself by not indulging in this time they had together? Why not just let things between them evolve however they were meant to evolve?

As long as they didn't affect Willy, he couldn't think of a good reason not to, and that was all there was to it.

He just had to hope that his hankerings weren't influencing his decision. At least not too much.

And that neither was his heart.

Given the family situation Clair had come from, big Sunday dinners were not things she was accustomed to. And the Brimley Sunday dinner was most definitely big.

Jace's mother and four of his five brothers were at the ranch when Clair, Willy and Jace arrived after a quick trip home to change out of their church clothes and into more comfortable things. And while eight people might not have been a huge number, the pure size of each member of the Brimley family made it no small gathering.

Junebug, Jace's mother—a smiling woman with pulled-back-in-a-bun white hair and a booming, no-nonsense voice—was six feet tall and at least three hundred pounds. Since not one of the Brimley brothers was under six feet, two inches of work-honed muscle, Clair felt slightly dwarfed as she was introduced to mother and sons.

Josh, Beau, Ethan and Scott.

Josh was Elk Creek's new sheriff and took a rash of joking about playing cops and robbers from Beau, Ethan and Scott, but they all seemed to accept Clair into their midst without missing a beat. None of them was shy. Each of them was warm, welcoming, charming and as handsome as they came.

Willy seemed to adore them all, referring to them as Unca Joss, Unca Beau, Unca Etan, and Unca Sott— Unca Sott taking his share of ribbing for that variation on his name. And as much as Willy adored them, the Brimley brothers seemed to adore him, passing him around like a football until he was giggling so hard he could barely catch his breath.

It was a pleasant day of good-natured teasing and competing over everything from basketball to Ping-Pong to pool to darts. Willy was included in it all and so was Clair, although she had to reject many of the invitations because she knew better than to try to match the brothers' pace and intensity in basketball or Ping-Pong.

She didn't display any talent at pool or darts, either, but she gave both her best try and was rewarded with the same kind of praise Willy garnered.

And the whole time she engaged in the Brimley's amusements or sat on the sidelines, two things kept running through her mind.

The first was how nice it was that a stranger's child had been taken in so thoroughly by the family. How nice it was that Willy was bathed in a warm glow of love from them all.

The second was that even though one of the Brimley brothers was as gorgeous as the next, the only time her pulse quickened and her senses went on the alert was when she watched Jace.

The dinner itself was a lively affair, and just as Clair began to think that no time in the Brimley household was calm, Beau suggested they bring out the home movies for Clair to see, and the whole group settled into the ample living room for that.

Willy gravitated toward Junebug then, asking to sit on her lap where he promptly curled up happily, contentedly, as if the huge woman really was his grandmother.

Clair felt a fresh stab of jealousy at the knowledge that it wasn't something her nephew would do with her, and she began to wonder if, on some intuitive level, Willy knew she was there to pluck him like a flower from a garden and whisk him away from all this, if that was why he kept his distance from her.

The home movies helped distract her from her more dour thoughts, though. The Brimleys had had their old reels transferred to video tape so there on the television she got to see Jace—and all the rest of the Brimley brothers—grow up.

Whoever had compiled the tape had done it by age group rather than in chronological order. All the brothers' first birthday parties came one right after the other, all their first days of school, and on up, giving her a peek at Jace and the other Brimley boys growing into the men they were now.

But, once again, it wasn't any of the other Brimleys who interested Clair. It was only Jace.

At least, it was only Jace until later years when another tall, lanky boy began to appear in many scenes with him, and Jace leaned over to tell her that the other adolescent was Willy's adoptive dad.

Everyone grew quiet when it came to those pictures and some of the fun went out of the room just before the tape ended and someone turned on the lights.

"Okay, maybe that *wasn't* such a great idea," Beau said into the silence that was left.

"Nah, it was great to see Billy again," Jace said, clearly the peacemaker in the family. "It just came as a surprise."

Then he glanced in the direction of the rocking chair Junebug had been sitting in with Willy, and Clair knew he was concerned at the effect on the toddler of seeing even the early images of the man whom Willy had known as his father before Jace.

But Willy and Junebug were no longer there. Or anywhere else in the room.

"Where'd they go?" Jace asked.

His mother reappeared as if on cue at that moment, coming down the stairs in the entryway. Apparently she'd heard enough to know that her eldest son was inquiring about her because she answered his question.

"Willy fell asleep so I took him up to your old bed. Are the movies over?"

"Just now," Jace said, and no one filled her in on those last scenes that had toned down the liveliness that had been the order of the day previously.

"I'd better get him home," Jace said then, sticking with the subject of Willy. "I didn't realize it was so late."

Junebug flapped a hand at him as if she were shooing away the suggestion. "Leave 'im. No sense disturbin' 'im when he's sound asleep up there and you'll be back here yourself first thing in the mornin' to work, anyway. He'll be fine. I'll make 'im his favorite hotcakes for breakfast."

"You know he's up before the chickens," Jace warned.

"There's enough of us around here to handle him. Don't worry about it," Ethan assured.

"He may wake up in the middle of the night wantin' the washcloth," Jace tried again. "There won't be any gettin' him back to sleep without it if that happens."

"We'll take care of it. Worse comes to worst we'll call you to bring it out," Scott said with a laugh.

"Yeah, just go. You can have a night off," Josh added as Beau nodded his encouragement.

Still Jace seemed to hesitate, but after a few minutes he conceded to his family and looked at Clair sitting beside him on the sofa. "I guess I'm outnumbered. I'll let him stay."

"It does seem silly to wake him up and take him out in the cold," Clair said, adding her two-cents worth.

That endorsement apparently cinched it for Jace because he stood and said, "Okay. Are you ready to go, then?"

It had been a lovely, family-filled day, which Clair had enjoyed, but she was definitely ready to go. Especially since going meant a little time alone with Jace.

"I'm ready," she answered, standing, too.

Jace got their coats, helping Clair on with hers before donning his own. She told the Brimleys how nice it had been to meet them all and thanked them for the day and the delicious food.

Then they said their goodbyes and went out to Jace's truck.

"Should I take out the car seat so you can have your own window for the ride home?" he asked, pointing with his chin toward Willy's seat that had occupied the passenger side since Clair had met him.

But if he removed it she had no reason to sit in the center of the truck's bench seat. Close to Jace. And while she knew she should have him rearrange things so she could be farther away from him, she just couldn't make herself do it.

"Then you'll have to put it back again," she said as if his convenience was all she had in mind. "That's too much trouble for just one short ride into town."

His smile was slow and amused, as if he knew what was really going through her head. But as he opened the driver's side door for her, he said, "Okay."

Clair slid in and only when Jace joined her and started the engine did she realize that this was the first time they'd actually been totally and completely alone. The first time Willy hadn't been in another room or asleep in the car seat. And for some reason that fact was slightly titillating.

Of course it didn't help that sitting beside her was a man who had more animal magnetism than any man she'd ever known. That his sharply chiseled face was breathtakingly handsome even in the dimness of the truck cab. That the scent of his aftershave lingered just enough to entice her. That his thick thigh was less than an inch away from hers and his big body gave off a heat all his own to chase away the chill of the night air, and that his hands—big, strong, adept, blunt-fingered masculine hands—were a sight to behold as they mastered the steering wheel and reminded her of what it had been like to feel them on her skin the night before...

The night before.

The night before when he'd so abruptly ended the caresses of those wonderful hands and told her he didn't think going any further was smart.

"I like your family," she said too brightly.

"They're good people," he agreed. "I think they liked you, too. It isn't every woman who's allowed down in the rec room, let alone into a game of pool with Ethan."

"I'm honored," she claimed with a laugh.

"We probably should have stayed down there rather than dredging up those old home movies."

Since Jace had made reference to what had sobered the men at the end of the day, Clair said, "How are you doing with that?"

"With seeing Billy on the tape?"

"Mmm-hmm. It seemed upsetting to everyone, and I'd think that would be more so for you."

Jace's expression was somber enough to let her know that watching his late best friend on tape *had* struck a nerve in him.

"Yeah, it was kind of tough," he admitted. "I guess nobody thought ahead and remembered that Billy showed up on those later portions of tape. I know there'll be a day when it will be okay to see him again, but it's too soon for that yet."

"The rest of the tape was good, though," she said in an attempt to lighten the tone and ease him out of thoughts of his late friend.

Jace seemed all too willing to put some effort into that himself because he managed a small smile and a glance at her with those denim-blue eyes that seemed to shine with life even in the barely lit truck cab. "My brothers were just tryin' to get to me by letting you see me as a kid and at my worst growin' up."

"I didn't see anything *too* bad," she teased. "Well, except for that cheesy mustache phase."

Jace pretended affront. "That was a great mustache."

"Ten whiskers and a shadow do not make a great mustache. And I'll bet a cracking voice went along with it and that's why no one could convince you to say anything through that part of the film."

"Actually the voice wasn't cracking much yet and I still sounded like a girl. A girl with a mustache," he informed her, laughing at himself. "And this is just what I needed—another witness to my puberty."

"It turned out pretty well so I don't think you have anything to be embarrassed about."

Clair wasn't sure where that had come from. Especially in the flirtatious, seductive tone that certainly hadn't been premeditated.

But Jace didn't seem to mind. He just glanced at her out of the corner of his eye this time and said, "Thanks. I've been admiring the results of yours all week, too."

That made her laugh again despite the fact that he'd used the same tone of voice she had, and she knew they were venturing again into territory that was off-limits.

"Besides," she said, "you were such a cute baby I hardly noticed the awkward stage."

"The bath scene," he guessed as he drove into Elk Creek. "I'm just grateful that they didn't catch me standin' up in the tub."

"Great chest action, though," she joked again even as she told herself to stop, that nothing good could come of bantering like this. Then, in an attempt to amend the tone of things, she said, "I also liked the birthday party with the pointy hat."

That made him flinch. "And the elastic strap that held it on and made me look like I had three double chins?"

"Very attractive," she deadpanned.

They arrived home then and Jace pulled into the driveway, coming to a stop and cutting the engine as he said, "Now don't be makin' fun. Even two-year-olds need their dignity."

"I think you have your parents to blame for bruising that," she said with another laugh at the memory of how silly he'd looked.

Even though the truck was turned off and he should have gotten out, he didn't. Instead he turned toward her and let his blue eyes scan her face. The expression on his didn't have anything to do with the joking they'd just been doing. It was more contemplative now.

"Guess I could walk you to your door tonight, couldn't I?" he said, again with that sensual undertone to his voice.

"I guess you could. If you wanted to," she added, trying to keep a lock on the disappointment she felt at the thought that her time with him was going to end so soon.

"We don't have the excuse of tuckin' Willy in to get you into the house."

"No, we don't."

"I could invite you in just for me, though," he said as if he were thinking out loud. Or maybe as if he were fishing a little for what her response to that idea might be.

"You could," Clair answered, leaving him wondering.

"What would you say if I did?"

She shrugged, trying to hold her racing pulse in check. "I'd say what about it not being smart?"

His supple lips eased into a grin. "Hoisting me with my own petard?"

Clair's only response was a questioning arch of her eyebrows.

"Today I've done a lot of thinkin' about just how dumb it might be to deny what's goin' on between us."

"And what would that be?"

"What's goin' on between us? Hell if I know," he answered with a wry laugh. "But somethin' has my blood boilin' all the time. Somethin' that's stronger than I am. Or am I the only one of us feelin' it?"

It crossed Clair's mind to pretend he was, that she didn't have any idea what he was talking about. Certainly it would put a damper on things and be safer in the long run if she did.

But it would also destroy this moment with Jace. This moment that it seemed she'd been yearning for almost since the day they'd met. And she couldn't make herself do it any more than she could make herself tell him to take out the car seat earlier and rob herself of any closeness with him. This man awakened things in her she didn't fully understand, but she wanted to…so much.

"I know there's something happening here, too. Something strong," she confirmed in a quiet voice. "I just don't know what it is, either."

Jace leaned in to rub the tip of his nose to the tip of hers. "I do know that I don't want to fight it anymore. Whether that's smart or not."

Clair nodded her understanding of that, her confirmation that she felt the same way in that, too. And on the upward nod Jace caught her mouth with his in a kiss that melted even the faintest hint of willpower in Clair.

"Do you want to come in?" he asked when that kiss ended, his forehead resting on hers.

"Yes," she whispered as if she were tempting fate

to say it out loud, ignoring every internal voice that wondered if she really should.

That seemed to be all Jace needed to hear. He got out of the truck and reached in a hand for her to take.

All hesitancy in Clair—what little there had been— fled and she slipped her hand into his, feeling a shiver of anticipatory delight when the thought flashed through her mind that soon his body could be slipping into hers in much the same way.

It sent her heart into a trip-hammer beat and brought every nerve ending, every sense, alive as it seemed that she was about to be granted what she'd wanted all along even more than she'd let herself realize. And that was saying something.

He took her up onto the porch and into the house without another word. Inside he didn't turn on a light as he closed the door behind them.

Staying there in the entryway, he shrugged off his coat and slipped hers off, too, with a stroke of hands that were careful only to brush her shoulders, tossing both coats away and letting them fall wherever they might as he seemed intent on studying her features even in the dark, on drinking in the sight of her with his eyes.

Then he put his hands on either side of her waist and pulled her in close enough to capture her mouth with his.

It was a test kiss. Light. Barely there. Until one of his hands left her waist to rise to her cheek, and he broke off that kiss only to tilt his head in the opposite direction and kiss her again.

That kiss was more serious and the hand that was still at her waist circled around to the base of her spine to bring her in even closer.

Clair's hands went up to his neck, to his head where his short hair bristled beneath her palm as he began to ease her away from the door. Backward. Deepening the kiss more with each step, parting his lips, sending his tongue to tease its way inside to hers.

She felt the wall come up against her back, and when it did Jace dropped his hand to her rear end and lifted her off her feet, till she was taller than he was and he could rain kisses along her jawbone to her neck and downward.

Down to the hollow of her throat, nuzzling in between the open collar of the black silk blouse she'd changed into along with her jeans after church.

Down even more to her breast where it strained for his attention through bra and blouse alike.

His arms were a sling for her to sit in by then and it seemed perfectly natural for her to wrap her legs around his waist, clamping them behind him and letting intimate portions of their bodies meet, jeans to jeans.

Clair did some teasing of her own then, kissing the thick column of his neck, touching only the tip of her tongue to the smooth satin of his skin until he came back to take her mouth with his again, open and hungry for her.

And with their mouths still attached, with lips and tongue still playing, Jace cupped her derriere in one hand and the back of her head in the other and carried her from the entryway into the living room. He dropped onto his knees on the sofa, the same site where they'd sat for hours together before, when what was now blossoming between them had only been simmering beneath the surface.

But tonight they weren't sitting side by side. Tonight he laid her flat on her back, keeping himself between her thighs while his mouth still possessed hers.

He found her breast with one hand. An adept hand that pulled her shirt free of her waistband and slipped underneath. A masterful hand that knew just how to tease her nipple into a tight little knot of desire that poked against the sheer lace of her bra. And she wanted, so much, to free herself of the fabric and feel his touch there.

But before that happened, out went his hand from under her shirt and he pushed himself up and away from her to stand suddenly next to the couch.

What flashed through Clair's mind was that he'd had second thoughts. That he was stopping this the way he'd stopped short the night before. That he'd decided yet again that this wasn't smart after all.

But then he leaned over and took her hand, gently yanking her to her feet, too.

"Not here," he said in a passion-raw voice that echoed with the sexual tension that had been building between them long before tonight, that was now coursing unchecked through their veins. "I want this to be right."

Relief washed through her that the only thing he'd

had second thoughts about was the place, and Clair was only too happy to let him lead her by the hand then, through the entryway again and up the stairs, where he paused to slough off first his boots and socks and then hers, leaving them in a trail behind them.

When they reached his bedroom Jace closed the door and stopped to take another long, heated look at Clair.

"You are so beautiful," he breathed as he slowly pulled his shirttails free and unbuttoned the front, leaving the ends to dangle around his hips, his chest tantalizing her from the narrow opening.

Then he caught her hand and took her to the side of the bed where he pulled the quilt and blanket down before he took her into his arms again.

His eyes seemed darker as he looked down into hers. His gaze was a caress in itself, of her hair, her eyes, her nose, her lips. A caress that slipped down to her neck, her shoulders.

Both hands moved up along her arms then. Up farther to her shoulders, to the back of her head and into her hair as he again took her mouth with his. But this time it was a slow, thoughtful kiss and a waltz of tongues that seemed to be getting acquainted with each other all over again.

Jace began to unfasten her blouse at a snail's pace, increasing her craving to be out of it with each button that slid through each hole. And when they were all undone he slipped the blouse off and let it fall to the floor at their feet.

Clair did him the same service, only too happy, only

too eager to press her palms to the mounds of his pectorals, to slide her hands up to his shoulders—learning the smooth, flawlessness of his skin stretched over hard, hard muscle as she followed a course down his arms to rid him of his shirt.

Jace stopped kissing her again as he unsnapped her bra, leaning far enough back to watch as he took the straps from her shoulders by index fingers hooked through them, letting them fall down her arms until the little lace nothing floated to the floor, too.

He stood there looking at her—at her breasts in the room lit only by moonglow—with a heated approval that left her unashamed, uninhibited, proud, even, to have him see her.

He filled each hand with one of them. Tentative at first, his touch grew more firm, more bold, more enticing as he let his mouth return to hers, this time wide open and plundering hers with his hot, insistent tongue.

Oh, but the man had miraculous hands! Kid leather against her bare breasts. Kneading, squeezing, molding, shaping them like a master sculptor working in his best medium. Knowing just the right amount of pressure, the right amount of tenderness, the right amount of teasing and tormenting until she was brought so alive with what he was doing to her that it was as if he were setting her on fire, and, all on its own, Clair's spine arched in answer, insinuating those engorged globes even deeper into his palms.

And then his hands were gone and all she could do was groan at the loss.

Jace chuckled, a low, primitive sound as he reached for the button on the waistband of her jeans, opened it, spread the zipper and smoothed the jeans, along with her panties, off her hips and down to be kicked out of the way.

In the time it took her to do that he'd dropped his, too, leaving them both totally, gloriously naked.

He laid her gently on the mattress then, lying with his body partially covering her side as he kissed her again more softly, letting little pauses lapse between each open-mouthed kiss so his tongue could trail along her lips instead, or so his teeth could tug at them.

Then he turned to nibbling her. Her chin, the line of her jaw, down the side of her neck to her collarbone and lower still until he reached her breast with his mouth.

At first only his teeth took her, oh, so carefully clasping her nipple and then flicking the crest with the tip of his tongue.

Clair couldn't help the second moan that escaped her throat as her whole body screamed for more.

And again Jace chuckled just before he released her nipple to take her breast into the warm, moist cavern of his magnificent mouth. Sucking, flicking, circling, it was a symphony of delights, each one tightening the silver cord that stretched down the center of her to that spot between her legs that craved him so badly she wasn't sure she could stand much more time without him.

She let her hands travel over his back, her fingers digging into his muscles, trailing the valley of his spine to its base and lower still, finding the taut curve of his derriere.

But that wasn't enough for her, either, and so she let one hand do a little more exploring. To his hip. To his thigh. Until she found him. Until she found the long, thick, steel shaft of his desire for her.

Jace was the one to groan that time. And writhe slightly, too, as she got to know him, got to know what he liked, what drove him wild.

He abandoned her breast and came fully above her, between her thighs, his big body fitting there as if it was meant to be there, as he kissed her yet again and eased himself into her by careful increments that only prolonged the pleasure of his body joining with hers.

He pulsed within her. Once. Twice. Merely flexing his hips, not really moving more than that at first.

But Clair wanted more. She was ready for more than that, so she pushed up into him in an initial thrust of her own.

Jace countered with a full thrust back, and so it began, still at his pace, though, as he raised himself up enough to lower his head to her breasts, flicking one nipple and then the other with the tip of his tongue as his lower half pressed deeply into her and withdrew with infinite deliberation.

But even he couldn't contain himself for too long before he increased his speed, before he was plunging ever deeper into her with a rhythm and pace that grew and grew until it was as if they were together in a race. A race up a steep, steep mountain of the purest delight. A race to the top of that mountain where a thunderstorm was building. A thunderstorm that erupted within Clair, complete with lightning so blinding she lost herself in the white-hot ecstasy that held her suspended, weightless and soaring all at once as she clung to him, as she arched her hips into him, as she took him so totally within her that they seemed melded together, his body to hers.

And then he, too, reached that peak and exploded to life, rigid and tensed above her, diving to the core of her and staying there, frozen, as his climax rippled through him and reverberated a second time through Clair, too, until each of them was spent and could do nothing but tumble from that high mountain to sink back to earth again.

But to an earth of cushioned, cloud-soft satiety that left Jace pressing her into the mattress as each of them worked to catch their breaths.

When they had, Jace pushed himself up and kissed her again, a kiss that sealed what they'd just shared.

Then he rolled to his back, taking her with him to lie against his side, her head on his chest, his kidskin hands rubbing her arms in a loving massage that lulled her and left her unable to resist the exhausted sleep that beckoned to her.

But as Clair succumbed to that sleep, she could hear the beat of Jace's heart, the pulse of life through his veins, and she couldn't help wondering how she'd lived so long without him, without what he could do to her.

Because every minute of her life before she'd met him suddenly somehow seemed so incomplete.

Chapter Ten

The sun was just coming up the next morning when a sleeping Clair rolled away from Jace's arms. It woke him up, just as her rolling away from him at 2:00 a.m. had. At 2:00 a.m. he'd pulled her back to him, kissing her bare shoulder. One thing had led to another, and they'd tired each other out again with a second round of lovemaking before they'd fallen asleep once more, arms and legs entwined and bodies so close together they were nearly one.

This time Jace didn't wake her. He remained lying beside her and propped his head on his hand so he could look at her.

From behind her he had a view of a sweet little spot right at the base of her neck where two tiny knobs of bone jutted out and seemed to beg to be nuzzled with his nose. But he refrained, still not wanting to disturb her so he could have this moment of studying her.

She had adorable ears, too, he realized as he scrutinized the one he could see. Small and perfectly curved in the midst of that curly, curly hair.

He was crazy about her hair. Dark, burnished, cherry wood silk, that's what it was. And so shiny it nearly shimmered.

There was nothing wrong with the bit of shoulder that peeked above the sheet, either. Straight and delicate.

And her skin? Ah, that skin! It felt even better than it looked, under his palm and against him....

He just had to touch her. He was itching to. So he reached over and took just one strand of her hair between his fingertips, rubbing it round and round.

And as he did, as he indulged himself in the sight of her sleeping so peacefully in his bed, something welled up inside him with the power of a tidal wave.

What had he thought in church yesterday morning? That when Clair left he'd have pangs? That he wouldn't be happy to see her go? That he'd miss her when she was gone?

Well, he'd just been kidding himself, he realized suddenly. Because in the instant that his feelings for her burst through the floodgates, he knew he was in deeper than he'd ever thought.

It knocked him for a loop, and he lay down on his back, staring at the ceiling to try to sort through what was happening to him.

How could this have sneaked up on him? he asked himself.

Sure he had known he liked her. That he was attracted to her. That he wanted to make love to her. That he wouldn't be glad about her returning to Chicago.

But this? This was more than that. Much more.

This was a feeling he hadn't believed he'd ever have again after Stephanie.

This was a feeling even stronger than what he'd felt for Stephanie.

Oh, man, he was in trouble.

He should have known. He should have seen it coming. He'd been enjoying her too much. He'd spent every day champing at the bit waiting for her. He'd liked having her around more than he should have. Her being there had even added a new element to tucking Willy in at night—a special, fuller element that had made it all the better. He'd hated it every time she'd left for the night. He'd been dreaming about her. He'd wanted her so fiercely it had been a driving need that most of the time had seemed greater than the need for food or water or sleep.

And yet he'd still fooled himself into believing he had some control.

Now he saw that that's just what he'd been doing— fooling himself. Because he hadn't had any control at all.

Damn.

She sighed in her sleep just then and wiggled around slightly, as if to get more comfortable, and Jace couldn't help letting his eyes wander in her direction again.

That was all it took for the tidal wave to hit him as forcefully as it had moments before.

Only this time, for some reason, when it did it also washed up thoughts of those old home movies they'd watched out at the ranch. Movies of his family. Working and playing. Celebrating. Growing up. Just being together....

It was what he wanted, what he'd always wanted—a family of his own. A wife. Kids. But he realized now just who it was that he wanted in that picture with himself and Willy and the other children he hoped one day to have. Who it was that he wanted to make a whole new set of home movies with.

Clair.

There shouldn't have been any surprise in that, either. Hadn't they been playing at being a family since she'd arrived in Elk Creek? A man, a woman and a child spending their days and evenings together, sharing their meals, relaxing on the sofa over wholesome movies and popcorn, looking after each other—that was all very family-like, wasn't it?

And hadn't it been as good as he'd ever thought it would be?

It had been. For him at least.

But what about Clair?

She hadn't seemed to hate it, that was for sure.

He knew when a person was hating the way they spent their time. He'd been witness to plenty of that in Stephanie. But Clair hadn't shown signs of any of that. She'd shown signs of the opposite, in fact, of enjoying herself even when she was at her most inept with Willy.

So maybe, unlike Stephanie, Clair might actually be willing to consider family life. With him. With him and Willy.

She had come all the way from Chicago to meet Willy, Jace reminded himself. To be a part of his life. And he'd seen how the loss of her sister—both when she'd told him about Kristin running away and when she had talked about her sister's death—had affected her. Family meant something to her, too. Something more than it had ever meant to Stephanie.

So maybe he had a shot.

Maybe he'd been wrong about Clair from the start. Maybe she wasn't as much like Stephanie as he'd thought she was. Maybe what had developed between them—and after the night they'd just spent he honestly believed something *had* developed between them that was deeper than either of them had realized before—maybe what had developed between them meant that they could have a future together. That they could raise Willy together.

Because he suddenly also knew that that was what he wanted. A future with Clair. A future as a family. A future raising Willy together.

In fact, the longer he thought about it, the better he liked the idea.

Especially if he'd been wrong when he'd decided Clair was too much like Stephanie to want Willy, if she really was in Elk Creek to get custody, then this was the solution to that, too. Clair could stay, make a life in Elk Creek with him, and then they'd both be there to raise Willy.

The whole thing just seemed right. A win-win situation. And maybe just what fate had planned, because the pieces seemed to fit so seamlessly—even if Willy might need a little more time to warm up to Clair.

And one thing was absolutely certain, Jace decided as he turned the idea over and over in his mind—Clair was what he wanted.

Clair and Willy and a lifetime together.

But he wasn't going to get that by lying there staring up at the ceiling and fantasizing about it. He was going to have to lay his cards on the table and let Clair lay hers on the table, too.

But that was okay.

Because how could anything this right go wrong?

Clair woke up to the sound of a shower running. For a moment she wasn't sure where she was. But then the scent of Jace's aftershave on her pillow reminded her of the night she'd just spent making love with him and sleeping in his arms.

The memory made her smile even though she hadn't yet opened her eyes. Of course, it didn't hurt that in her imagination she also pictured Jace showering, that magnificent body she'd come to know so well naked under the spray of water, droplets dappling his ruggedly handsome face, those wonderful hands soaping up smooth, masculine skin...

Maybe she should surprise him and join him...

But just as she began to consider that, she heard the shower turn off, and it occurred to her that if he came out of the bathroom dressed or even in a robe, she didn't want to be without anything on.

So she scrambled out of the bed, snatched up her panties and the shirt he'd worn and discarded the night before, slipping them both on.

The shirt was huge for her. It was a navy-blue flannel that was as soft on the inside as it was on the outside, but the arms went well past her fingertips, and the tails reached her knees.

Being nearly overwhelmed by it was worth it, though, she thought as she buttoned the front and rolled the sleeves up to her wrists, because it retained the clean scent of Jace's aftershave, which wafted around her, enticing her all over again and making her wonder if maybe she *should* have waited for him in bed—naked in bed—so he could join her there again.

But she didn't have time to act on that because just then the bathroom door opened and out stepped Jace.

He had a towel wrapped around his waist, one corner tucked in at his side, and nothing else. That glorious torso was bare beneath the kiss of the sun coming in through the window. Clair wanted to cross the room and slide her palms over every inch of tight washboard stomach, perfect pectorals, broad shoulders and bulging biceps.

"Hi," he greeted with a pleased smile the moment he caught sight of her.

Obviously he'd had the same thought about closing the distance between them because that's just what he did, coming to take her in his arms, pulling her to him for a good-morning kiss.

"I was going to make you breakfast and bring it up here before I woke you," he told her as she wrapped her arms around him and pressed her cheek to his chest.

"That's okay. I'm not hungry." At least not for food. But *he* was another matter altogether....

"I want to talk, then," he declared.

Not what Clair had had in mind in lieu of breakfast. But something in his tone sparked her interest.

"Okay," she agreed, standing straighter so she could look into his freshly shaven face, letting the pleasure of just that ripple through her.

"I want to talk about us," he said. "And Willy. And why you really came to Elk Creek. And you stayin'."

Nothing like cutting to the chase.

"Oh," Clair said in response, her posture growing involuntarily stiff suddenly at the introduction of the subject matter.

Jace must have felt it because he squeezed her slightly, as if that might loosen her up again.

It didn't help.

"I've been awake about an hour and doin' a lot of thinkin'."

"Apparently."

"Thinkin' about how I feel about you. About how nice it's been havin' you around. How much fun we've had. You know, up until yesterday, I was pretty worried that you'd come to Elk Creek to try to take Willy away.''

He said that so easily, as if it didn't really concern him at all.

''*Is* that why you came here?'' he asked amiably enough.

Clair considered lying outright, something she'd avoided doing since her arrival in the small town. But what would be the point of that now?

''Yes, that's why I came here,'' she admitted.

Jace nodded but didn't seem alarmed. Actually it almost seemed to please him.

''Why didn't you worry about it until yesterday?'' she asked.

''I got to thinkin' that maybe that wasn't the case. That you were too much like Stephanie, and Stephanie definitely didn't want kids, so you probably didn't, either, and weren't here to take Willy away. That maybe you really had just come to meet him, to make contact, but that was about as far as it would go.''

That seemed like a curious thing for him to have thought about so cheerily.

Then he added, ''Today I'm countin' on you provin' me wrong.''

Clair's heart began to pound, but for the first time since he'd started to cause that reaction in her, it didn't have anything to do with being attracted to him or wanting him.

She was still so incredibly attracted to him and wanted him so badly that she could hardly think straight—especially with him naked except for that towel—but it was something more serious that was speeding her pulse. Something far less pleasant.

"I guess I just did prove you wrong since I told you I came to Elk Creek because I *do* want Willy," she said very quietly, hoping to soften the effect.

Jace nodded. "Which means you *do* want kids in your life and you must be ready to make a change in it to accommodate that," he concluded.

"Yes," she confirmed tentatively, unsure where he was going with this.

Then she found out.

"So how about stayin' in Elk Creek and raisin' Willy together, you and me?"

She couldn't be sure what "together, you and me" meant, but the other portion of that was what set off alarms in her. Alarms so loud she had to move out of his arms, away from him, as she said, "How about staying in Elk Creek? I can't stay in Elk Creek. What would I do here?"

"Okay, we'll talk about work *first*," he said, more to himself than to her and with an edge that let her know he wasn't wild about the order. "There are a lot of folks around here who telecommute. We might be a one-horse town but we do have phone lines and computers. Maybe you'd have to give up being an account executive and take a pay cut, but you could probably still do something in advertising—write ad copy or something. And less money and no title would just be a trade-off for havin' a life. Isn't it worth that?"

"I have a life. I have a great apartment. A great job. Friends," Clair said defensively, thinking suddenly that while Jace might look a whole lot different—and better—than Lyle, underneath they could be more alike than she'd thought. Alike enough for Jace to be standing there calmly suggesting that she give up all she'd achieved just because he had some sort of whim.

"But you don't have Willy. Or me," he pointed out in response to her list of all she *did* have.

"I planned to take Willy back to Chicago with me," she said carefully, not sure how to address any thoughts of doing the same with Jace.

"Why? So you can pass him off to a nanny or a baby-sitter or a day-care center? Or am I missin' something, and you're thinkin' of quittin' your job there to devote yourself to him?"

"Of course I wouldn't quit my job. My job is the most important thing to me—" She cut off her own words, hating the way they sounded, knowing what chord they were striking in him. "Not more important to me than Willy is," she amended then. "But you have to understand, Jace, my job is the one constant in my life. I had too many years of upheaval before that. It's my safety net. It means independence to me. And I like it. I'm fulfilled by it. Excited by it. I couldn't just not do it anymore. Besides, I have friends who work just the way I do and still manage to raise children."

"Not well."

"That isn't true."

"It is for you, Clair. You aren't the greatest at parenting, even when that's all you're doing."

That cut her to the quick, even though he was right.

"Taking Willy back to Chicago with you would be the worst thing you could do," Jace continued. "You said yourself that you work six days a week, and more nights and Sundays than you can count. That it feels more like you live in your office than your apartment. If you had Willy he'd feel like whoever was taking care of him was his mother, not you. And what about saying that it seemed to you that my having Willy around while I worked was a 'hindrance'? You were talkin' from your own standpoint, and we both know it."

Clair was even more on the defensive by then. She could feel it but she couldn't fight it. Any more than she could keep herself from saying, "I can go to court and probably be awarded custody if you won't agree to my taking him."

Anger erupted in Jace, too. She saw it in the big hands that jammed through his short hair and in the jaw that clenched and unclenched.

"I'm not talkin' about what some judge might say," he nearly shouted. "I'm talkin' about what's best for Willy. Or did so much of that Lyle-I-want-things-my-way-no-matter-what rub off on you that you can't see beyond yourself at all? That you don't care about anything but yourself?"

"That's not fair."

"Fair? I'll tell you what isn't fair. It isn't fair for a little boy to be ripped away from people he knows and loves and trusts to be around people he doesn't know. To be stuck in a day-care center when he could be with me, outside in the fresh air every day. It isn't fair for him to be raised by someone who will spend more hours at her job than with him.''

Jace threw up his hands, shaking his head, breathing a disgusted sigh. And before Clair could say anything, he added, ''I honestly didn't think this would play out like this.'' Then he seemed to stab her with those denim-blue eyes of his. ''And what about you and me? What about last night? Was that all nothing?''

Oh it was so much more than nothing!

But it couldn't be everything...

''No, it wasn't nothing,'' she said. ''But—''

''But what? Thanks for the tumble but now I'm going to take you to court and tear up your life and wreak havoc on Willy's, too? What about all that upheaval you're so damned determined to spare yourself more of? Is it just okay to submit Willy to it instead?''

That struck home. Clair hadn't thought about it like that. And she didn't want to.

''It would only be the one time. I'd make sure he had stability after that.''

''One time? This is a boy who's already been handed off by his birth mother and lost the parents he knew to a car accident. Now you want to uproot him? At least losin' Billy and Kim didn't take him out of the home he knew, out of the town, away from every single living soul he's familiar with. How is it 'just one time' after all that?''

''He should be with his blood relatives. His real family.''

''What blood relatives? You and a grandfather who's already failed as a parent himself? And I don't see him here. I'll bet he couldn't care less if he ever sets eyes on his grandson.''

Clair couldn't deny that, because Jace had hit the nail on the head—her father hadn't even wanted her to come, he hadn't wanted her to bother with Willy any more than Lyle had.

''Willy will have me. I'm his aunt, after all,'' she said, hating that that was the best she could come up with for her own side of this.

''He would have you if you stay here, too,'' Jace said again, his voice lower, deeper, more reasonable again. ''And he'd have everything else he should have along with you. But you'd have more. I'd have more. We'd have each other.''

It was a tempting scenario—the three of them together....

But even in the midst of her imagining it, a little voice in the back of her mind kept shouting that this was Lyle all over again wanting it all *his* way, wanting her to give up absolutely everything to accommodate him.

''No,'' she heard herself say before she realized she was going to.

''No?'' Jace repeated. ''No, you don't want to stay here? No, you don't want to try and make a go of things with me? No, you don't want to raise Willy together?''

''Not if it means my having to sacrifice my whole life to do it, no,'' she confirmed, sounding even to her own ears as if her back were against a wall and panic was speaking for her.

The answering look on Jace's face tied her stomach into knots. She knew what he was thinking. That she was no different from his ex-wife.

And in that instant she saw something harden inside him. She saw him draw himself up and become her adversary.

"I won't let you take Willy," he stated flatly, as if that were the only thing at issue, as if her refusal of all the rest had put an end to that portion of the discussion. A final end to them and what had developed between them.

Clair swallowed the lump in her throat, wishing she wasn't being bathed in that cold stare, wishing that she were still seeing the warmth his eyes had held for her until that moment.

But he wanted too much of her. Just the way Lyle had. Too, too much...

"You know you could always move to Chicago," she ventured feebly.

Jace just shook his head, and she knew without his saying it that the idea was lame.

Clair squared her shoulders and tried to convince herself that the man she was facing—the same big, strong, unbelievably handsome, caring man—was now her enemy. And she said, "I guess it'll be between lawyers then."

"Bring 'em on," he dared her, arching one eyebrow in challenge.

There didn't seem to be anything left to say. Clair grabbed up her scattered clothes and took them with her out of his room, out of his sight, only slipping on her jeans under his shirt and her feet into her shoes before she walked out of his house completely.

And as she did she tried to find comfort in the fact that, for the second time, she'd been strong enough not to give up everything for a man.

The only problem was, this time losing the man made her feel as if she'd just lost everything....

Chapter Eleven

Rennie Jennings was in her bathrobe, sitting on her couch with a cup of coffee and the morning newspaper when Clair let herself into Rennie's house a few moments later.

Clair wasn't happy to come face-to-face with her hostess when she was dressed in Jace's shirt, carrying her own clothes in a wadded up bundle and obviously just out of Jace's bed. It was no way to be seen by anyone, let alone by the town minister's sister.

And it didn't help that at sometime on the dash across the yards, a waterfall of hot, unwanted tears had begun to streak paths down her cheeks.

"What's the matter? Are you all right?" Rennie asked the moment she glanced up at Clair, alarm resounding in her voice.

"I'm fine," Clair lied, as if it would throw her hostess off the track when there was so much evidence to the contrary.

"You're not fine. You're crying. When I saw that your bed hadn't been slept in last night I thought good things must have happened next door. But now—did something bad happen? Is Willy okay? Jace?"

"Willy and Jace are fine."

"Then what's wrong?"

"Just a bad start to the day," Clair said vaguely, wiping her cheeks with her fingertips as if the tears were merely dust, all the while trying to stanch the flow.

"Come and sit down and talk about it," Rennie suggested, patting the sofa cushion beside her.

"You don't want to hear my tale of woe," Clair demurred, reluctant to confide in a stranger and thus trying to make light of what felt anything but.

"Sure I do. Come on. Maybe it'll help."

Clair was acutely aware of the fact that Rennie was more Jace's friend than hers. But still she liked the other woman, and it occurred to her that maybe Rennie could give her some insight into Jace that would make for better results than she'd accomplished on her own.

"Come on," Rennie urged again with another pat of the sofa. "I even have a clean tissue in my pocket," she added as if that were an incentive.

It made Clair smile slightly, and for some reason sitting with Rennie and telling her the entire tale suddenly had some appeal.

She set the bundle of clothes on the coffee table, sat

on the opposite end of the couch and accepted Rennie's tissue, drying her eyes, blowing her nose and sniffing back any more tears.

Then she told her hostess the whole story, sparing no details, even when they didn't shed a flattering light on herself, and bringing Rennie up to just moments before, when she and Jace had argued.

"You came to Elk Creek to take Willy away from Jace?" Rennie asked when she was finished, as if that part of what Clair had told her was the most unthinkable.

"Willy *is* my nephew," Clair pointed out needlessly.

"Well, sure. But Jace...Jace is so amazing with Willy. And Willy is so crazy about him."

"In other words you think I should just bow out and leave Willy with Jace," Clair said, wondering if maybe she'd made a mistake after all by talking to Jace's neighbor about this.

"Do you see it differently?" Rennie asked. "Because what I see is a little boy who's come through a pretty big trauma without much fall-out because he has Jace."

"But Jace isn't his family. *I* am."

"I don't think Willy cares much about bloodlines."

"No, he doesn't care about bloodlines now, not when he's only two and a half years old. But he may care someday. And in the meantime he can't make decisions for himself."

"He seems to have decided that he loves Jace. That

Jace can take the place of his parents. To Willy that makes him family.''

"But I'm *really* his family. I can give him things Jace can't. I can keep his mother alive for him.''

"Maybe you're looking for a way to keep his mother alive for *you*,'' Rennie said gently.

Clair didn't respond to that. It tweaked a nerve that was still too raw. Instead she said, ''What if something happened to your brother and his wife? Would you want Lissa with someone totally unconnected to you or to any of your family? Would you want to be just some outsider from far away who calls once in a while or visits? Or would you want to be a part of her life?''

Rennie conceded that point with a shrug. ''I'd want to be a part of her life, but a part that didn't hurt her in the process. Wouldn't you even consider moving here so Willy could have both you *and* Jace? Because, I have to admit, that seems like a pretty good solution.''

"Would you be willing to give up everything?'' Clair demanded, feeling defensive again.

"I guess not if that's how I looked at it.''

"How else would you look at it?''

"Well, if something happened to my brother and his wife and I discovered Lissa with a great guy who I also happened to get hung up on, I'm trying to think of why I *wouldn't* take the chance to be with Lissa and that man if that man asked me to be.''

"Who said I was hung up on Jace?''

Rennie glanced down at Jace's shirt and barely suppressed a smile. "Nobody had to say you were hung up on Jace. It's in the air."

"Okay, I like Jace. He's a good man. A great guy. He's gorgeous. He's nice. He's funny. He's fun to be with. He's incredible with Willy. He's—"

"And you only *like* him?" Rennie cut in with a laugh.

"He's also asking me to give up my whole life," Clair countered. "To leave a job I've worked hard at. To leave my home. To leave my friends. My father—"

"All right, that's a lot. But he's offering a lot, too."

Clair wasn't exactly sure *what* he was offering, because she hadn't let him get far enough to lay it out. But apparently Rennie assumed Jace was offering more than just coparenting.

"I only know," Rennie said, "that if I were in your shoes I'd give some consideration to what Jace was proposing. Yes, you'd be looking at a big change—"

"A *huge* change."

"A *huge* change. But in the first place, if you really want what's best for Willy, I'd say that what's best for him is to leave him with Jace. And in the second place, you'd get Jace, too."

"Are you sure you don't have a thing for him yourself?"

Rennie laughed. "Absolutely positive. But just because I'm not attracted to him doesn't mean I don't recognize how terrific he is. And apparently so do you or you wouldn't have been singing his praises a minute ago. Or spending last night with him."

"It doesn't matter how terrific he is if the relationship is all one-sided. If I have to make all the sacrifices for it."

"Initially you might have to make all the sacrifices. But it isn't as if that will go on indefinitely. Or is that what you're figuring?"

Well, yes, Clair guessed that *was* what she'd been figuring. Because that was the way her entire relationship with Lyle had been, and she knew that, had the relationship continued, she would have had to go on sacrificing and adapting and being the only one to give anything up. In fact, the only way the relationship *could* have continued was on Lyle's terms.

"Once it starts out that way—"

"Jace isn't like that," Rennie said, cutting in again, not even allowing Clair's rationalizing. "He's one of the most giving men I've ever met. He's taken over the raising of someone else's child, for crying out loud. And he's left his own home to do it so Willy could be in familiar surroundings. He's been all about making sacrifices and changes to help that little boy. Plus he sacrifices his time and energy for anyone who needs him. Me, our neighbors, his friends, his family. This is not a person who thinks the world revolves around him. Sure, out of necessity, he may be asking you to make all the changes at the beginning, but I don't see any reason to believe he'll expect that down the road."

Clair couldn't argue with that because she knew it was true. It just hadn't been something she'd taken into consideration, because she'd only been thinking about the here and now. About what she would have to give up to move to Elk Creek permanently. About Jace being like Lyle...

Rennie seemed to realize she'd struck a home run and didn't need to say any more because she stood, taking her coffee and newspaper with her.

"Would you like me to fix you some breakfast?" she offered then, out of the blue. "Maybe you could think better on a full stomach."

"No, thanks," Clair answered, her head spinning and the distraction of all her thoughts echoing in her voice. "I think I should take a shower."

"Good idea. Clear away the cobwebs."

Clair stood, too, following her hostess as far as the hallway that led to the guest room and going off by herself then as Rennie headed for the kitchen.

But Clair took Rennie's words along with her.

Was she more concerned with keeping Kristin alive for herself through Willy than keeping Kristin alive *for* Willy? she asked herself once she was behind closed doors.

Yes, there was probably a part of that in her reasons for coming to Elk Creek, she admitted. She'd loved Kristin. She'd nearly raised her. And she missed her terribly. She'd missed her terribly since the day Kristin had disappeared. To have the opportunity to see even a shadow of her sister in Willy every day? She couldn't help wanting that.

But at what expense? a little voice in the back of her mind asked as she slipped out of Jace's shirt, out of her own things, and went into the bathroom for her shower.

Was she willing to meet her own needs at the expense of her nephew's?

If she was, then *she* was like Lyle.

That was not a possibility she appreciated. But once the ball began to roll in that direction it gained some momentum.

Wasn't she also being like Lyle if she was inflexible? If she was intractable?

She didn't want to admit that, either, yet under the circumstances it was difficult to deny. She certainly hadn't been willing to bend when it came to Jace's proposal for a future for the three of them.

But even adapting to fit Lyle's needs had never been as extreme as the change that would face her if she made the move all the way to Elk Creek. A change that big was fraught with the same kind of instability she'd sworn to protect herself from, the same kind of instability she'd suffered as a child. Was it any wonder it had triggered panic in her?

Clair stood beneath the spray of the shower and just let the warm water flow over her, face and all. But it couldn't wash away the thought that if she forced the custody issue, if she succeeded in taking Willy away from his home, away from Jace, she would be inflicting the same kind of upheaval on Willy that she was trying to spare herself.

And she'd be putting her own needs ahead of his. She'd be sacrificing his sense of security, his sense of stability, in order to preserve hers.

Lyle. Lyle. Lyle.

But there was an alternative, she told herself as she turned off the water.

She could just go home. And maybe that was what she *should* do. Maybe she should just leave Willy with Jace, leave everything as it was before and merely keep long-distance contact with her nephew. Then she wouldn't disrupt Willy's life. She wouldn't disrupt her own.

But offering herself that option did a strange thing. It made her feel empty inside. Lonely. Desolate. It made her heart ache far more than the breakup with Lyle had. The simple thought of going back to Chicago by herself, of leaving Willy behind, of leaving Jace behind, of going on with her life without them, was suddenly unbearable.

"I guess that's what you get for being inflexible and intractable," she muttered. Lyle had lost her, and she would lose Willy and Jace.

But while Lyle may not have cared enough about losing her to do anything to stop it, she cared a whole lot about losing Willy and Jace. She cared so much that she suddenly knew with clarity that it wasn't what she wanted. No matter what.

What she wanted was just what she'd had since arriving in Elk Creek—Willy, Jace, being with them each day and each night.

Even if it meant giving up everything else.

What had Jace said this morning? *What about last night? Was it all nothing?*

And what had she thought? That it hadn't been "nothing" but that it couldn't be everything.

Now she wasn't so sure that was true. Could what was between her and Jace—could a family made up of Jace and Willy and her—be everything to her? Could it be the trade-off Jace had talked about that made all the change, all the upheaval, all the sacrifice, worth it?

It seemed as if it could.

Besides, the more she thought about Jace and the sort of man he was, the more she knew that Rennie was right when she'd pointed out that all the changes she would need to make were initial changes, that it wasn't setting the course for the whole relationship with Jace. Jace definitely wasn't someone who would expect her to do *all* the adapting all the time, the way Lyle had.

No, the longer she mulled over the whole thing, the stronger was her belief that she could have a good life with Jace. A wonderful life with Jace. That she could have just the life she'd always dreamed of.

It just had to start out with her making the first sacrifices, the first compromises.

At least, she assumed a life together was what he'd been talking about.

As she stepped out of the shower something else— something far less encouraging—flashed through her mind. The memory of Jace's expression when he'd finally accepted that she wasn't going to agree to move to Elk Creek, that she wasn't going to agree to sharing in Willy's upbringing, when she'd threatened him with lawyers.

His handsome face had turned cold. Hard. Angry.

She'd thought that she was looking at an adversary. Someone who was suddenly nothing *more* than an adversary....

A shiver shook her and it had nothing to do with the dampness she was drying from her skin.

What if she'd ruined things with him? What if she'd destroyed his feelings for her and now he'd rather battle for Willy than have her in his life?

But this is Jace, she thought. *Kind, considerate, compassionate, understanding Jace....*

Who had already been hurt deeply by a woman Clair knew was like her in some ways.

She'd just have to sell him, she told herself, working to push past the fear and trying to put Jace in the same category as a valuable client who had so far only seen mediocre ad campaigns from her. She'd have to win him over in spite of the similarities to his ex-wife. She'd have to let him know just how ready and willing she was to make one more major change in her life.

She'd have to let him know just how much she loved him.

Because she *did* love him, she realized. She loved him more than she'd ever loved any man. And she loved Willy, too. She loved them both enough to do anything to be with them.

"He's going to think I'm crazy," she told her reflection in the mirror as she thought about knocking on his door a scant few hours after running out on him to say, Never mind, if you'll still have me I'll stay after all....

But whether or not he thought she was crazy, whether or not he was still angry with her, going next door and telling him she wanted what she thought he'd been proposing was exactly what she had to do.

Because *not* doing it meant not having Jace. Not being with Willy.

And *that* was just not something she could settle for....

Chapter Twelve

Clair had to wait longer than she'd expected to talk to Jace. By the time she'd dressed, done her hair and makeup and returned next door, he was gone.

She'd considered going out to the ranch, tracking him down, but she had no idea who might be with him there, and the idea of doing what she was intent on doing in front of his mother or brothers seemed like a bad one.

So she waited. And worried. And paced. And rehashed Jace's every word a hundred times, searching for encouragement in what he'd said before she'd rejected him.

Rennie was with her most of the day and that helped. Once Clair had confided her decision to the other woman, Rennie couldn't have been more supportive. The minister's sister assured Clair that she was doing the right thing. That it would all work out. That Jace's anger and coldness of the morning were only natural and would disappear just as soon as Clair told him she was staying.

And while Clair hoped it was all true, another part of her worried that it wasn't. She even tortured herself with thoughts that maybe Jace had picked up Willy and taken him away someplace where she'd never be able to find them. Where she'd never see either of them again.

But just after suppertime, as Clair stood vigil at Rennie's picture window, she finally saw Jace's truck turn the corner at the end of the block.

"Here he comes!" she called in an excited voice, despite the fact that Rennie was sitting on the sofa just behind her.

Taking her cue, Rennie set aside the paperwork she'd been doing, sprang to her feet and followed Clair as she rushed out of the house.

They'd had long enough today to hatch a plan, and neither of them needed to say a word to put that plan into action. So, as they hurried across the yards, the only thing Rennie said was, "It'll be okay. Just keep your eye on the prize."

The prize was exactly what Clair's eye was on. Both eyes were on Jace as he rounded the truck he'd just parked in the driveway so he could take Willy down from his car seat.

He looked as if he'd had a hard day. His chiseled face seemed haggard and lined. And he did not seem happy to see the caravan of two that charged him as he and Willy came back around to the driver's side of the truck.

He just watched them coming, without greeting either of them, and Clair thought that poor Rennie was having to be the recipient of his dark scowl by association.

"Hi," Clair said when she and Rennie reached him, hoping her greeting sounded warm enough to let him know she hadn't come for a confrontation over Willy, which she sensed was what he thought.

Jace merely inclined his head to acknowledge the greeting, but he didn't answer it.

"Can we talk?" Clair asked.

"I don't have anything else to say," he told her with a chill in his voice.

"Wennie, I dots a dood wock," Willy said then, seeming oblivious to the tension that was shooting between Clair and Jace.

Clair tried not to take offense at Willy's ignoring her in favor of a neighbor, and kept her focus on Jace.

"How about if you go over to Rennie's house and show her your good rock?" Clair suggested to the toddler, proud of being better able to translate his mispronunciations than she had been at first.

"Is it okay if he comes with me for a while?" Rennie asked Jace.

"Should I be worried that this is a kidnapping conspiracy?" he asked her, as if he'd believe Rennie's answer more than he could believe one from Clair.

"I've only conspired to give you guys a little while alone," Rennie assured him.

Jace nodded his consent. "Okay. But don't make me break down your door to get 'im back," he warned.

"Don't worry," Rennie said as she ushered Willy back the way she and Clair had come.

Neither Jace nor Clair said anything while the sound of Rennie's voice was still in the air. They just remained locked in a stare that left them at odds.

He wasn't going to give an inch, Clair thought. But since she wasn't sure she deserved even that much, she didn't let it discourage her.

"I suppose you want to go inside," Jace said when Rennie and Willy were out of earshot, his tone less than hospitable. "But I should tell you right now that if you think for one minute you can convince me to hand Willy over to you, you're wrong and I won't have my time wasted listenin' to it."

"That isn't what I have to say," Clair told him. "But I would like to go inside."

Jace led the way, and as Clair followed and tried not to feast on the sight of his perfect posterior, she wondered if he was treating her to a dose of bad manners on purpose.

But once they were at his front door, his manners kicked in again and he held it open for her to go in first.

The house was chilly; apparently he'd turned the heat down for the day. Clair just hoped that was the only heat that was turned down and that she could raise Jace's temperature as easily as he had turned up the thermostat.

"What is it you want to talk about?" Jace asked her then, standing barely a foot inside the arch that connected the entry and the living room, his hands on his hips, his weight slung more on one hip than the other, his denim-blue eyes as cold and hard and angry as they had been earlier in the day.

"You put me into a panic this morning," she began from the center of the room where she'd stopped and pivoted to face him. Then she went on to tell him how his idea about her staying in Elk Creek had affected her and why.

"I wouldn't expect that our whole life together would be about you giving in to me," he said when she'd laid out the whole list of things she'd had to concede to Lyle. "I'm not going to dictate when and what you eat or every movie we see or every TV program we watch or what you should read. I wouldn't want you not to have any friends of your own, and I can't imagine making you only see 'em when I'm not around."

"I know. Rennie pointed out that my perspective was limited and that's part of what got me here tonight."

"What's the other part?"

"I realized that you were right and that I couldn't do to Willy exactly what I was trying to save myself from—a big move, so much change, upheaval. I worked hard to get myself away from my father's control so I could have stability, and I guess I was hanging on so tight to it that it didn't even occur to me that I was going to inflict the same thing on Willy."

"And now."

"I know I can't do that to him. I can't take him away from you. You're so good with him and he adores you. Besides, I could never replace you. Not for him or for me," she added in a soft voice.

"I wondered if we were ever going to get to the you-and-I portion of things. Or is there a you-and-I portion?"

"There's definitely a you-and-I portion," she said. "At least I hope there is. I nearly threw myself into a tailspin just thinking about not having you in my life."

"There's that 'in your life' thing again. You said it about Willy at the start of this—you wanted him to be a part of your life, you wanted to be a part of his— and here it is again. It leaves me not too sure exactly how far it goes."

"It goes all the way," she said, not intending the innuendo that was in her voice. But there he was, standing tall and muscular and magnificent, his rug-gedly handsome face etched with lamplight, his shoulders so broad they seemed able to carry the weight of the world. And she was having trouble keeping her mind from wandering to thoughts of how it had felt to be in his arms the night before, to how her naked body pressed to his felt. To having his hands on her. To having him inside her....

"Explain to me just what 'all the way' we're talkin' about," he said. As if he'd been reading her mind, a slight smile curved just one corner of that mouth she was dying to have kiss her…everywhere.

"I guess maybe you should explain to me first what you meant this morning when you were talking about me staying in Elk Creek, about our raising Willy together."

"I was talkin' about you marryin' me," he said easily enough.

Clair couldn't suppress a smile of her own as relief washed over her. Well, partial relief, anyway. She still didn't know if the offer had been taken off the table.

"Then I'm talking about going all the way to that. Unless you've changed your mind…"

"You'd give up your big-deal job in Chicago, move to Elk Creek—for good—and make a new life here with me?"

"Yes," she said, amazed at how wonderful that suddenly sounded.

"And you wouldn't look back? You wouldn't pine for it all and end up high-tailin' it out of here later on?"

Clair knew from where his doubts stemmed and that he was thinking about the ways in which she was like his ex-wife. But there was one big way in which she wasn't like his ex-wife that he'd overlooked.

"Don't forget that it's stability I've craved since I was a kid myself, Jace. Roots. Staying in one place to build my life. Making the move here is a huge thing for me, and once I've done it I'm here to stay. Like it or not. It's what I need."

"I'll like it. But will you? Elk Creek isn't Chicago."

Clair had no problem answering that, either, because she'd had all day long to think about it. "Elk Creek is a nice place. Small, but nice. And you were right about the telecommuting. I can't be an ad executive from here, but I can still work. I can freelance or maybe start something on my own. But the most important thing to me now is you and Willy. I thought maybe I'd make you two my number-one job."

"You've got me, but Willy'll take some work."

Clair met Jace's eyes with hers, seeing the warmth that was in them once again, reveling in it. "Do I have you?" she asked quietly.

He crossed the room to her then, clasping his hands on either side of her hips to pull her up close to him. "You have me, hook, line and sinker," he said just as quietly.

That was when Clair felt fully relieved. And more. She felt her heart swell and her eyes flush with tears. Happy tears this time.

Seeing them made Jace smile but only for a split second before he leaned in to kiss her.

His lips meeting hers ignited the same flame they would have lit if the events of the morning had never happened. That same passion still simmered just beneath the surface in them both.

Before she had time to think about it, clothes were flying, and mouths were open, and tongues were playing while hands explored and relearned and aroused.

Tonight the sofa was as far as they got. Tonight the

urgency—maybe to reseal what had suffered a tear—was even greater than the urgency of the previous evening. And neither of them could do anything but ride the wave right there and then. A grand wave of sensation that united them more deeply than either of the other two times they'd made love, that brought them each to the ultimate peak of pleasure and then let them drift back to earth on angel's wings, body to body, heart to heart, soul to soul, arms and legs entwined in a tangle of perfect bliss.

And when they could breathe again, when the pounding of their pulses wasn't all they could hear, Jace said, "Will you marry me, Clair?"

"Yes," she answered without hesitation.

"Good. Because I'm so much in love with you that I can hardly stand it."

She nuzzled her head into the hollow of his shoulder as she lay atop him, their bodies still one. "You aren't standing at all," she joked.

He pushed up into her one more time, an intimate nudge. "Not what I wanted to hear in answer to the first time I tell you I love you."

She smiled against his chest. "I'm so in love with you that I can hardly stand it, either. Or did you think I was willing to throw my whole life away and start over with you just because I like you a little?"

"It's nice to hear, anyway," he told her in a voice left raspy from lovemaking.

"I do love you, Jace," she said more solemnly then, just in case he had any doubts.

"Good. Because I do love you, too," he said the same way.

For a long while they just stayed like that, connected, contented, holding each other, wrapped in the warmth of that love.

Then Jace said, "How long do you think Rennie will keep Willy?"

"She's probably already wondering what's going on over here that's taking so long."

"Guess we should go get him, then."

"Guess we should."

But neither of them moved.

"Think we could get a license tomorrow and be married by the weekend?" he asked after another moment.

"You're really in a hurry."

"I can't have you stayin' here nights until we're legal. What kind of an impression would that make on our boy?"

Our boy—the words made Clair's heart swell even more.

"No, we wouldn't want to make a bad impression on him," she agreed.

"And I can't wait much longer than that."

"Neither can I," she whispered as if it were shameless to admit how much she wanted him even now.

But she was sure she'd find comfort in knowing that in a few days the three of them would be together. Forever. And that was all that really mattered.

"You'll have to help me get to be better with

Willy," she said a few minutes later, when they were still just lying there.

"It'll come," Jace said without a bit of concern. "What did I tell you before? Things happen the way they're supposed to, and Willy warmin' up to you will happen, too. Just give it some time."

That she could do, now that there was no rush on it.

"I love you, Jace," she said yet again, for no particular reason except that the feeling had welled up inside her so much she had to tell him.

"I love you, too," he said without missing a beat. "And so will Willy. You'll see."

She knew he was right.

But then everything about this was right—that was something else she knew.

Deep down and without a doubt she knew that it was right for the three of them to be together no matter how convoluted the path had been to get there.

And together the three of them would keep alive in their hearts so many of the people they'd lost. All the people it had taken to bring them together in the first place.

Because, in spite of the tragedies that had led to this moment, there had always been love and caring and a drive to do what was best.

What was best for Willy.

And now she and Jace would go on striving to do that same thing.

Which wouldn't be too hard, Clair thought.

Because she knew that Jace was definitely the best.

For Willy.

And for her, too.

And that the best of all possible lives would be what the three of them would share.

*   *   *   *   *

Beloved author
Sherryl Woods
is back with a brand-new miniseries

THE CALAMITY JANES

Five women. Five Dreams.
A lifetime of friendship....

On Sale May 2001—DO YOU TAKE THIS REBEL?
Silhouette Special Edition

On Sale August 2001—COURTING THE ENEMY
Silhouette Special Edition

On Sale September 2001—TO CATCH A THIEF
Silhouette Special Edition

On Sale October 2001—THE CALAMITY JANES
Silhouette Single Title

On Sale November 2001—WRANGLING THE REDHEAD
Silhouette Special Edition

"Sherryl Woods is an author who writes with
a very special warmth, wit, charm and intelligence."
—*New York Times* bestselling author
Heather Graham Pozzessere

Available at your favorite retail outlet.

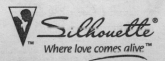

Where love comes alive.™

Visit Silhouette at www.eHarlequin.com   SSETCJR

CALL THE ONES YOU LOVE OVER THE HOLIDAYS!

Save $25 off future book purchases when you buy any four Harlequin® or Silhouette® books in October, November and December 2001,

PLUS

receive a phone card good for 15 minutes of long-distance calls to anyone you want in North America!

WHAT AN INCREDIBLE DEAL!

Just fill out this form and attach 4 proofs of purchase (cash register receipts) from October, November and December 2001 books, and Harlequin Books will send you a coupon booklet worth a total savings of $25 off future purchases of Harlequin® and Silhouette® books, AND a 15-minute phone card to call the ones you love, anywhere in North America.

Please send this form, along with your cash register receipts as proofs of purchase, to:
In the USA: Harlequin Books, P.O. Box 9057, Buffalo, NY 14269-9057
In Canada: Harlequin Books, P.O. Box 622, Fort Erie, Ontario L2A 5X3
Cash register receipts must be dated no later than December 31, 2001.
Limit of 1 coupon booklet and phone card per household.
Please allow 4-6 weeks for delivery.

I accept your offer! Please send me my coupon booklet and a 15-minute phone card:

Name: _____

Address: _____ City: _____

State/Prov.: _____ Zip/Postal Code: _____

Account Number (if available): _____

---

097 KJB DAGL
PHQ4012

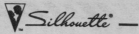

If you enjoyed what you just read,
then we've got an offer you can't resist!

Take 2 bestselling love stories FREE!

Plus get a FREE surprise gift!

Clip this page and mail it to Silhouette Reader Service™

IN U.S.A.	IN CANADA
3010 Walden Ave.	P.O. Box 609
P.O. Box 1867	Fort Erie, Ontario
Buffalo, N.Y. 14240-1867	L2A 5X3

YES! Please send me 2 free Silhouette Special Edition® novels and my free surprise gift. After receiving them, if I don't wish to receive anymore, I can return the shipping statement marked cancel. If I don't cancel, I will receive 6 brand-new novels every month, before they're available in stores! In the U.S.A., bill me at the bargain price of $3.80 plus 25¢ shipping and handling per book and applicable sales tax, if any*. In Canada, bill me at the bargain price of $4.21 plus 25¢ shipping and handling per book and applicable taxes**. That's the complete price and a savings of at least 10% off the cover prices—what a great deal! I understand that accepting the 2 free books and gift places me under no obligation ever to buy any books. I can always return a shipment and cancel at any time. Even if I never buy another book from Silhouette, the 2 free books and gift are mine to keep forever.

235 SEN DFNN
335 SEN DFNP

Name	(PLEASE PRINT)	
Address	Apt.#	
City	State/Prov.	Zip/Postal Code

* Terms and prices subject to change without notice. Sales tax applicable in N.Y.
** Canadian residents will be charged applicable provincial taxes and GST.
   All orders subject to approval. Offer limited to one per household and not valid to current Silhouette Special Edition® subscribers.
   ® are registered trademarks of Harlequin Enterprises Limited.

SPED01   ©1998 Harlequin Enterprises Limited

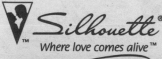